Her Guardian Angel Cowboy

Texas Knights Series, Volume 1

Janalyn Knight

Published by Janalyn Knight, 2021.

Chapter One

With her son, Dusty, asleep in the bedroom, Jayme Bonner picked up the mail and shuffled through it. Her gaze froze on the last, unexpected envelope sporting the logo of the Texas Department of Criminal Justice. Collapsing on the couch, her mind in lockdown, she feared what this might mean.

Hands shaking, tensing her muscles for impact, she ripped opened the letter, growing instantly lightheaded as blood drained from her face. Dirk Blacke still had six years left on his sentence, but they'd let the man out of prison. When she'd been notified of the hearing, she had been assured there was little chance he would be released because of his list of infractions inside. Unable to face being in the same room with the hateful man, she hadn't attended. Blacke had attacked her and tried to kill her. Now that he was free, he'd keep his promise to finish her off.

TWO WEEKS LATER, JAYME opened her grit-filled eyes to the first light of dawn. Dew dappled the windshield, and she rubbed her cold hands together to warm them. Dusty lay across the seat, his mop of golden curls in her lap. Even after sleeping another night in her old truck, her boy never complained. He

1

tried so hard to make things easier on her. At eight years old, he cared more for her needs and feelings than any grown man ever had.

After leaving her last job in the middle of the night, without giving the foreman more notice than a note left in the darkened barn, she'd run fast and hard from the hateful convict on her trail. Dusty was her life; she'd do whatever it took to protect him. Faced with this threat, running was her best—her only—option.

In the rearview mirror, the dark circles visible under her eyes were testament to her exhaustion. She massaged her temples. They'd traipsed from one small North Texas town to another, stopping in at every feed store and gas station asking for leads on work. There were three more months of school left this year, and Dusty was falling behind. Every day lost increased the pressure.

She was a ranch hand, but being a woman looking for a man's job was no easy thing. A tip the day before had seemed promising, but it turned out to be an offer for more than ranch work after the guy had gotten an eyeful of her. And she damn sure didn't want a job like that.

Lord, please let me have some luck today. My boy needs to be in school. She was down to her last fifty dollars, and that didn't go far when you were driving an old Chevy truck. She hated that Dusty had been living on the cheapest food she could buy for the last couple of days. She clenched the steering wheel until her knuckles cracked. Something had to change.

Starting up the truck, the engine loud in the quiet of the sleepy town, she patted Dusty's soft cheek as he turned over and lay on his side.

She drove out of the little parking lot of the saddle store in Throckmorton and headed down Highway 380. There were some sizeable ranches up in Haskell and Stonewall counties. Surely Howelton, where she was headed, held more promise than the other towns they'd been through recently.

After thirty minutes of driving past green wheat fields running all the way to the flat horizon, she came to the small farming community. The donut shop coming up on her left was more than she could resist. Her son needed a treat, and he loved donuts more than anything in the world.

The truck's engine stopped, and the constant vibration from the old engine stilled. In the silence Dusty sat up and knuckled his face. He spied the display through the picture window and turned wondering eyes her way.

She nodded her head and grinned.

Throwing his slender arms around her neck, he squealed like a baby pig and jiggled his short golden curls.

She laughed and tickled him. Her son had a way of lifting her heart, even on the toughest days.

He shrieked, "You're going to make me wet my pants."

"Come on in, honey. Use the restroom while I get your donut and some coffee."

"I'll be quick."

He hauled his cute little butt into the store and asked where the bathroom was. She shut her door, her own rear end sore from having slept sitting upright night after night, and walked inside.

A plump woman with kind, gray eyes stood behind the ancient wood-and-glass display. "Good morning," she greeted Jayme. "How can I help you?"

The aroma of coffee and fresh, hot bread filled the warm air. Jayme's empty belly rumbled loudly, and she crossed her arm over her stomach. Had the store clerk heard?

The woman grinned. "Sounds like you got here just in time, hon."

She'd eaten very little in the past few days after giving Dusty most of what she could afford. It was no wonder her stomach was complaining. Jayme smiled tentatively and pointed at the fluffy glazed creations. "I'll have a large black coffee and one of those donuts, please."

The woman poured her coffee, snapped a tight lid on the tall cup, then slipped a donut into a bag. Dusty skipped back into the room with an excited smile.

Jayme paid for her purchase and gave him his breakfast. "Here you go, buster. Enjoy."

Dusty peered inside the small brown bag and frowned. "What are you going to eat?"

She swiped his hair out of his eyes. "I'll have something later."

He stared at the old hardwood floor, all the joy in his treat gone. "You're hungry too."

Her little man, always looking after her, trying to be the man of the house. "Just eat your donut, hon. We'll find something for me soon. This town has great vibes. There's bound to be work here."

He stood still, his face stubborn.

Oh hell. She turned toward the counter to order another donut.

The lady handed her another bag. "No charge. I swear you deserve one for raising such a sweetheart."

Tears burned Jayme's eyes, and she lost track of what the woman was saying.

Dusty tugged on Jayme's sleeve. "Mom, did you hear that?"

"What, honey?"

"She wants to know what kind of work you're looking for."

Jayme quickly wiped at the corners of her eyes. "Thanks for asking, ma'am. I'm a ranch hand, and I'm desperate for a job. We've been looking a while, and that old truck drinks gas like a drunk on Saturday night."

The woman sighed and shook her head. "My name's Noreen. I'm telling you now so's you'll know who to cuss when you leave this job in your rearview mirror. You'll find work out at Ward Ramsey's place. That ornery son-of-a-gun can't keep help for nothing." She tore off a piece of register receipt and wrote down directions to the ranch.

Jayme thanked her for her kindness as her belly worked its way into a knot. She didn't have it in her to trust men much, but her managers had never been jerks. No matter what this Ramsey was like, though, she had to try.

A HALF HOUR LATER, Jayme and Dusty passed the cattle guard under the wrought-iron sign of the Double R Ranch. Peering down the road, she didn't see anything like a ranch house in the distance. After driving a mile or so past wheat fields and grazing Black Angus cattle, she came to a mesquite pasture. As they eventually rounded a bend, an old, fort-like, adobe-and-rock ranch house appeared. Driving past it, they took a hard right at a thick copse of mesquite trees and prickly pear cactus, and a well-built steel barn came into view. A dark-blue Ford truck was parked in front.

She pulled up next to the truck and ruffled Dusty's hair. "Stay here and don't make a peep. You know the drill, right, hon?"

"Yep. Nobody wants a kid problem. I'm not here until you say so."

Her heart ached for him. She hated that he felt he was a problem.

"Well, I wouldn't put it exactly like that, but yeah, you've got the idea."

He wadded up their nighttime blanket into a pillow, lay down on the seat, and closed his eyes.

Hope swelled her chest for the first time in a while. She got out and stood for a few seconds, composing herself and saying a little prayer. The morning sun was kind to her skin, not yet blazing as it would be later in the day. God, she needed this job so badly. With a deep breath, she strode into the barn.

Though the doors let in the sunlight, no one was inside. Pitchforks and shovels hung in an orderly row, and boxes and bottles were stacked neatly on shelves—signs of a well-run ranch. She breathed in the light manure scent of healthy cattle and a whiff of the round bale of coastal hay near the rear. Heading down the aisle, she eyed the dark cows in some of the stalls to her right. The double doors in the back were open.

A clear, masculine voice came from the small pasture behind the barn.

She exited the building and laid eyes on the source of the sound. Goose bumps ruffled the hairs on her arms. If this was Ramsey, he couldn't be further from the cantankerous old coot of Noreen's description. Jayme stared at a strikingly handsome man, armed with a stock whip, moving some cows and calves toward a corral.

Her gaze roamed over his lean, broad-shouldered frame. His sculpted, sun-browned jaw clenched, leading to a scowl on full, sensual lips. He tossed dark hair from his forehead, and she caught her breath at an unwelcome ache in her core.

As soon as the cattle were in the corral, the gate slammed. She backed inside to the cool shade of the barn, waiting for him to enter.

Walking in, he hardly spared her a glance, though that frown of his was firmly in place.

She moved toward him, her heart beating like a drum. "Mr. Ramsey?"

"Yep."

"I'm Jayme Bonner. Noreen in town said you might be looking for a hand. If you are, I'd like to talk to you about the job."

He grabbed a pitchfork and pulled hay from the round bale, then turned and looked her up and down. "For who?"

With a gulp, she steeled her resolve. This was always the hard part. "Me. I've been working ranches for years. I'm a damn good hand."

He turned his back to her and forked more hay. "Don't need a woman here. I need someone strong who can work hard."

She fidgeted from one foot to another, then caught herself. *Please let him see through his prejudice and give me a chance.* "Well, that's me. My old bosses gave me reference letters. Call them. They're in Texas. They'll tell you how hard I work and that I'm dependable."

Without turning around, he shook his head. "You're just not big enough. Can't lift what needs lifting. Now, git."

Stepping closer to him, she kept a note of desperation out of her voice. At least, she hoped so. "Please just try me. I'll prove I can do the job. Or take a minute to read one of the letters. It'll tell you that I'm up to anything you put me to." *Oh, God, this has to work. I'll beg if I have to. Dusty deserves better than what he's been getting. I'll do whatever it takes—well, almost.*

She held out a reference letter, the paper crisp against her fingers. *Take it, come on. Give me a chance.*

Pausing in his work, he turned around, his piercing stare shooting straight through her. He reached for the letter and read it in silence. Finally, he looked up and studied her.

Warmth stole through her insides as he stared. Damn, the man was good-looking.

Then he grimaced, aiming that gaze of his over her shoulder.

She stood still, begging God to please help her land the job.

He shifted his hard gaze back to her. "I'll give you a try for two weeks. Then we'll talk. There's a cabin. It needs some cleaning. Last assh—hand was a nasty son of a—" He puffed out a sharp breath and shook his head, muttering, "I'll regret this. I know I will."

Her knees went weak. Her mighty God had come through again. And not every ranch job came with a place to stay. Without it, the truck would have been home for her and Dusty until she could afford the first month's rent somewhere.

She threw her hand out. "I promise you won't."

Ignoring her hand, he stepped past her. "Follow me."

Trailing Ramsey outside, her pulse racing with elation, she snuck a peek at her truck. Little smarty-pants was still tucked away. The blue Ford backed out as she climbed in and started her engine.

She tailed Ramsey, her hands gripping hard on the steering wheel, as he followed the drive around and down about half a mile. A small, old-fashioned, faded-white house overrun with scruffy grass and weeds appeared. Behind it glimmered a stock pond. It probably also provided water for the house since wells were rare in this part of the country.

Ramsey pulled up to the little house and got out.

She parked and walked over to stand near him.

He motioned to the house. "This has a key. It's not locked since I didn't clean it yet. Payday is every other Saturday."

She nodded, then headed toward her truck and opened the door. Heart in her throat, she said, "I need to mention something." Dusty sat up, and she helped him out.

"Dammit! You didn't say anything about having a kid!" Ramsey hollered.

Before she could speak, Dusty shouted, "Don't yell at my momma! It's mean!"

The man jerked his head back and blinked, then took a closer look at Dusty, eyeing his thin little frame up and down. Ramsey nodded his head slowly. "You're right. I shouldn't have yelled at your momma." Tipping his hat to Jayme, he climbed into his truck, backing up and heading down the road toward the barn.

She let out a long breath and squeezed Dusty's shoulder. "Thanks for standing up for me, son."

The house had good bones, with wood floors and a large picture window in the small living room. The place held very little furniture, but she could live with that. She'd learned not to acquire more than would fit in the back of her truck. Taking whatever a bunkhouse offered was something she accepted. This house was a pigsty, though. They'd have to clean it before bedtime.

There was something else they needed to do first, though. Loading Dusty back into the truck, they went by the school to register him, her mind full of positive thoughts about her new job and the rancher who set her pulse to racing.

They got back to the little house and she started to work, first unpacking their clothes into the dresser in the single bedroom. Her prized possession, Dusty's current school photo, went on top. It was the only decoration that traveled with her wherever she went.

Thankfully, there were some cleaning supplies under the kitchen sink, and she spent the afternoon scrubbing the house. A quilt her mother had made before Jayme's birth went over the back of the worn couch, finally making the old cabin feel like home.

That night, sleep evaded her. Noreen had been right. Her boss was a hard man—just like her father. She fiddled with the covers and turned over for the second time. Remembering working with her cold, dominating father, she bit her lip. This job could be painful.

A LOUD SOUND WOKE HER. Her head shot up. What time was it? She checked the clock on the bedside table. Eleven-thirty. Her cell phone pealed again. She glanced at the caller ID. Unknown. Hoping Dusty didn't wake, she punched the green button and whispered, "Hello?"

"Hi there, bitch."

Blacke! She gasped, cold terror racing through her limbs.

"That's right. It's me. You think you can hide? Think again. I'll find you. And jail gave me lots of time to think about what I'll do to you when I do. You and me? We're going to have some fun. Sleep good now." He hung up.

She lay there, clutching the phone, unable to move. Prison hadn't changed him at all. He was coming for her. She shivered, suddenly icy cold and vulnerable.

She moved to the couch and covered herself with the quilt her mother had lovingly made. Its usual calming magic held no power tonight. How could she protect herself? How could she protect Dusty? The man was brutal, insane, when he was angry. His attack was proof of that. She'd never felt quite as alone as she did right this moment.

She needed a plan. She'd get a new number. Her phone felt tainted now that his horrible voice had come through it. Running her hand through her hair, she clenched a handful, pulling it tight. But wouldn't it be smarter to let him call her? He might slip and give her clues to his whereabouts or what he was planning. God, could she bear to hear his voice again? Let him threaten her?

They'd never spoken on the phone before. And in the years since he'd been in prison, she'd never considered that, as senior hand at the ranch, he might have had access to her phone number. She'd tried to put all thoughts of him and her rape as far from her mind as possible. That had been a mistake.

WARD RAMSEY REACHED into the refrigerator for a cold beer. After being fidgety all afternoon, now he couldn't sleep. A house over 150 years old was never truly silent. It creaked and popped and whispered all night long. He sat down in his recliner, needing the comfort of the room with its smoke-stained rock fireplace and worn leather furniture. Why in the hell had he offered the woman a job?

The antique mantel clock ticking was the only real sound once he settled in at night, unless Skippy snored. His Australian Shepherd, asleep near the sofa, lifted his head and looked at him.

He heaved a sigh. He'd been telling the woman no, he didn't need her, and the next thing he knew, he was showing her the cabin. Shaking his head, he groaned. He had actually hired a female ranch hand.

When he'd walked into the barn and gotten a clear look at her, a hot jolt of desire had surged through every inch of him. She was the first woman to get his blood pumping in a very long time. The direct way she stared at him with those wide, green eyes surprised him. He felt the heat from that gaze pulsing all the way to his boots. She must have found that being gorgeous wasn't a bonus when working on a ranch.

And hell, she had a kid. He took a long swallow of beer. How had he not seen *that* coming? He'd expected her to let some kind of dog out of the truck. He couldn't have that boy running around this place. A weight landed hard on his chest as he glanced at the photos on the mantel, something he rarely did.

One was his wedding picture, taken all those long years ago. Elizabeth had been so beautiful and carefree that day. He shut his eyes and drew in deep, shuddering breaths.

He looked up again. Apparently this was a night for scourging himself. He gazed at the other photo. His three-year-old son, Caleb, laughed at him, reaching out with his little palm open. Panting, Ward leaned forward and put his face in his hands, resting his elbows on his knees. The accident should never have happened. He should have been with them.

He clenched his fists and groaned softly. If he had been driving, he could have prevented the wreck. But he had put the damn ranch ahead of his family one too many times. Elizabeth and Caleb had paid the ultimate price.

He thought of calling Casey, his best friend, but then chucked that idea. Talking about his loss would only make him feel worse.

No, having the woman and her son here wouldn't work. However, she had two weeks. As a man of his word, he'd keep it. Then she was out of here.

JAYME, JITTERY FROM lack of sleep, was at the school when the doors opened the next morning. She sat with Dusty while he ate breakfast in the cafeteria. Then she walked him to his new class and met his teacher, leaving the woman her phone number for emergencies. Now she just had to get permission from her hard-ass boss to pick up her son from his afternoon bus.

It was eight o'clock when she drove up to the ranch. Ramsey skewered her with those brown eyes of his as she entered the barn.

"You're late," he snapped. "Don't make it a habit."

Shaky all over after the threatening phone call last night, she found it hard to face her boss. Resorting to a detested nervous habit, she tucked a bit of loose hair behind her ear. "I took Dusty to his first day at school."

When he didn't make a comment, she chewed on her lip, then asked, "What time do you want me here in the mornings? You didn't say yesterday."

"Seven-thirty. Start the feeding if I'm not here yet."

She could do that. Dusty's bus picked him up at a little after seven. "Sounds good."

"I guess you ride?" he asked.

"Yes, sir, and rope."

"Pull calves?"

She nodded. "Yes."

He grunted and scratched his cheek. "Any experience on tractors?"

She nodded again. "John Deere, yes, sir. I can run a dozer and a backhoe, too."

He narrowed his eyes, sizing her up. "Guess you mend fence all right, too?"

"Yes, sir. I can string a damn tight fence, as well."

"Castrate?"

"Yes, sir." She frowned. What was this? Twenty questions? Was he trying to trip her up?

He kept on. "Done any well or pump work?"

"No, sir."

"I was beginning to wonder," he grumbled.

"What's that?"

"Nothing."

Sucking in her bottom lip, she kept her peace. This man, the one who revved her pulse, was exasperating. But, in truth, he had the right to grill her about her work experience. Couldn't he be a little less grumpy about it, though?

He threw his thumb over his shoulder. "Go hook up my truck to the flatbed. We'll buy a load of feed this morning."

The trailer was on the truck when Ramsey walked over and got in the passenger side. He checked the lights' connection on the trailer first.

It was jury-rigged, and she'd had to work out the wires. He must have figured she wouldn't get it right. He'd figured wrong, and the look he gave her had some respect in it.

He said, "Drive back out to the main road. I'll tell you where to go when we get into town. I get my stuff at Howelton Feed."

Jayme glanced sideways at her boss, all too aware of his tall, hard body blocking the sun on the other side of the truck.

Ramsey drew quite a few interested looks, which he ignored, on arriving with an unfamiliar woman driving his rig. He left her in the truck while he did his business, but when he came back, he tossed a new light connection for the trailer on the truck seat. "You know how to put that on?"

"Sure do."

"Good. You can do it when you get some time this week." After that, he ignored her.

Which was fine with her. She couldn't imagine what kind of conversation this grouchy man would find interesting.

When they returned to the ranch, he had her reverse up to the feed room. Shoving open his door, he nodded at the trailer. "We'll unload. I'll toss them to you."

"Sure thing." Her boss was a man of few words all right. Turning her head to avoid watching his muscular shoulders bunch as he hoisted the feed, she grabbed the bag he sent flying her way.

His gaze tracked her closely as she easily caught and stacked the bags in the feed room. What was he thinking? Was he realizing how capable she was of doing this job, or was he sizing her up as a woman like other men had? She hoped it was the former. It wasn't good to have the men she worked with thinking of her as female, especially her boss.

She tossed another bag onto her pile. What made such a handsome man wear that cold, hard look anyway? He was so unfriendly. She hoped he got that stick out of his butt soon.

With both of them working, the job wasn't so bad. While she closed up, he pulled the flatbed over and unhooked it by the other trailers, then strode back into the barn where she was awaiting his next orders.

Being tall and strong for a woman, she usually felt like one of the guys. But something about this big, rock-hard man made her feel small and surprisingly feminine. Not exactly what she wanted while she worked. Clearing her throat, she looked into the pen beside her.

Hands on his hips, Ramsey frowned and pressed his lips into a thin line. "We'll take an early lunch. Be back here in an hour."

She nodded as she watched him stride off. What was this attraction? How could she feel drawn to the man when he obviously couldn't stand the sight of her?

A FEW MINUTES LATER, standing in her tidy little kitchen, she drank four glasses of water, her stomach growling. That would have to hold her until this evening. Her cupboards were bare. The remaining fifty dollars in her wallet needed to last as long as possible.

No way would it carry her two weeks. She had to ask for an advance, but not on her first day. And how she dreaded the asking. Standing on her own two feet was something she prided herself on. Even growing up with her father, she'd always felt alone. Caring for herself was a habit, and asking for help came hard. But taking care of her boy was the most important thing in her life.

Maybe after work she could stop and buy a few things at the little grocery store in town—beans, milk, eggs, and such. She qualified for free breakfasts and lunches at school for Dusty. Dinner was her only worry now.

She took off her boots and socks and lay on the old bed in the small, stark bedroom, thanking God for finding her this job. Instead of resting, however, her heart ticked like an over-wound clock. The menacing phone call haunted her.

After his first violent attack, Dirk Blacke would finish what he started. Nowhere felt safe. With her stomach burning, she turned over, staring at the age-stained wallpaper and smelling an old house that had been damp too many times. She focused on one thought—she had to protect Dusty and keep herself alive.

Tamping down her fears, she clenched her fists. She was doing all she could. Maintaining a low profile and staying here in Howelton, far away from South Texas where Blacke knew to search, was a good first step. Tonight she would write to her last boss, telling him where to mail her final paycheck and asking him to keep her location secret. He was a good man, and she knew she could trust him.

Pulling the extra pillow against her belly, she squeezed her eyes shut. The weight of her responsibility crushed her into the lumpy mattress like a thick layer of concrete. Sleep had been hard to come by since she'd received the parole letter. Her meager precautions seemed meaningless in comparison to the destruction Blacke could rain down on her.

She needed to ask about meeting Dusty's afternoon bus, but this morning hadn't seemed like the right time. A tough guy like her boss would not be thrilled. Time was running out.

SHE KEPT A CLOSE WATCH on the time and was back at the barn in an hour, dreading the talk she needed to have with Ramsey.

The blue truck arrived shortly after.

The early afternoon sun glared into her eyes. Her hands were trembling, dammit. Taking a breath, she clenched her fists and met Ramsey as he headed toward her, locking gazes with him. "The bus will drop Dusty off at the end of the lane at ten minutes after four. I have to be there to pick him up. He does his homework while I work."

Ramsey stared, his eyes squinted nearly shut. "What if you're somewhere that you can't be there at ten after four?"

Dammit. He wasn't going to make this easy. She hardened her mouth. "I don't plan on being somewhere that I can't get him at that time."

He thrust his head forward, squared his shoulders, and parted his lips to say something.

I can't back down. I have to make this work. She cut him off. "Look, you're my boss, and I know you can tell me where to go and what to do. I'll work long hours and do every hard, nasty chore you assign me on this place, but the one non-negotiable is that I pick up Dusty when he gets here. I'll go right back to what I was working at afterwards. None of my bosses have ever had a complaint. I hope you'll give me a chance, too." She looked into his eyes, searching for some give, a hint that he might understand her need.

He stared, a dark frown on his face, and then nodded slowly. "Two weeks."

Chapter Two

The rest of the week wore Jayme down to the ragged edge of her strength. Her boss pushed her hard every day, as if trying to make her quit. She wasn't about to give up. She needed this job too badly. They worked until dark every evening, which this time of year came about seven, and the grocery store in Howelton closed at six. That meant that her first night had been spent driving forty-five minutes to the twenty-four-hour Walmart in Stamford. Dusty had eaten a dry sandwich on the way home and fallen asleep. After carrying him into bed, she felt, not for the first time, like a horrible mom.

Working until seven was too damn long for a ranch hand, and she was sure Ramsey knew it. The man had the advantage. She'd trusted him to be fair when she took the job and hadn't asked what time he'd turn her loose in the afternoons. She wouldn't give him the satisfaction of bitching, though. Let him try to run her off. She was a lot tougher than she appeared—and sure as hell tougher than he gave her credit for.

Come Friday night, Ramsey, with his usual frown, stopped her as she was leaving. "We work Saturdays, but not a full day. You'll be off at one-thirty."

"I'll be here." She gritted her teeth as he walked away. Her body, which flushed with secret heat in his presence during the day, was such a damn traitor. That man didn't even know she existed, unless he turned one of those scowls on her. Grimacing, she headed for her truck.

Some ranches worked their hands all day Saturday, so she was pleasantly surprised. Dusty would have to come along with her. One thing was certain; Ramsey had better be nicer to her son than he was to her.

THE NEXT MORNING, AS the sun was beginning to warm the windows of the blue Ford, Ramsey, Jayme, and Dusty drove the fence line at a pasture near Knox City, hoping to find where their bull had gotten out. Jayme glanced at her boss. He stared out the windshield with his jaw clenched. She sighed. Nothing she did seemed to soften the guy up. She tried hard to do her chores to perfection, hoping to impress him, maybe earn his good opinion. Anything to take that look off his face. Her bosses had always appreciated her and her good work. His attitude was really starting to bug her. What was it going to take to change his mind?

Her boy rode in the center, all buckled up, asking questions about things he saw inside the truck. "Mr. Ramsey, what do you use this rifle for? How come you carry it around with you?"

Ramsey's grimace came as no surprise. But at least he hadn't scowled at her son. That would have pissed her off big time.

The man took a deep breath and answered, "I keep it in case I see wild hogs out in my fields, tearing up my wheat."

"Oh... You have a CD player. How come you don't have any CDs?"

Ramsey took another long breath. "No time for music."

"Oh... Do you have any kids?"

Sharp intake of breath. No comment for a while, then, "Why don't we play the quiet game? You sit quiet, and I'll time you. See how long you can stand it."

The boy frowned. "Okay. Starting now?"

"Yep." Ramsey ignored both of them until he found the hole in the fence.

She spent the time hoping Dusty kept his mouth shut.

The truck rolled to a stop, and her boss switched it off.

"How long was it?" Dusty piped up.

"What?"

"How long was I quiet?"

"Oh." He checked his watch. "Seventeen minutes."

"Sure felt longer. I don't want to play that game anymore."

The guy wasn't very good with kids. Speaking of kids, why didn't he answer that question about children? She glanced at him. The man was inscrutable, as always. His dark hair, too long at the nape of his neck, curled at the ends, giving him a boyish look. And that strong profile and square jaw would make a movie star scream with envy.

Little tingles made her heart dance. She pinched her lips together. There she went again. In another lifetime, she'd be happy to be so attracted to this man. But he was her boss—and, oh yeah, he hated her.

The guy pissed her off, too. He was rude when he didn't need to be, and she didn't deserve it.

After fixing the hole in the fence, they fed cattle and finished taking a head count, then headed back to the ranch. They weren't breaking for lunch since they were knocking off early.

At noon, Dusty patted Jayme's leg. "I'm kind of hungry, Momma." She hadn't been able to afford any snacks when she went to the store. A sharp pain stabbed her chest. She was such a crap mom.

"Honey, can you hang in there a little while longer? We'll be home soon."

Ramsey reached into the glove box and handed her son an oats and honey granola bar, which she noticed was in pretty bad shape.

It was the last thing she'd expected the man to do. Maybe he had some human kindness somewhere under all that grump after all.

The boy grinned all over. "Thanks, Mr. Ramsey."

No answer, of course.

They made a quick round, checking the wild hog traps near the house. A couple held a bunch of the anxious, treacherous animals. After hooking up the sixteen-foot trailer, they headed back to load them. Dusty minded her, staying in the safety of the cab while she and Ramsey tended to the dangerous job of transferring the pigs to the trailer.

A guy near Abilene bought the animals, and the meat went overseas as a delicacy. The biggest boars went to an exotics place for hunting.

She had another unpleasant task ahead of her before quitting time, and she was dreading it like hell. Once they unloaded the hogs, she sent Dusty on over to her truck. Her hands trembled as she prepared to face her boss. Would he give her a look of disdain when she put her question to him? God, she couldn't bear that. But her last paycheck from her previous job hadn't arrived yet, and she was desperate.

With her fists jammed in her pockets, she stared Ramsey in the eye. "I have a favor to ask. I'm flat broke, and I'll be out of food for my son soon. My truck's on empty, too. If you're able, I need an advance of $120 on my paycheck." Tiny muscles in her arms quivered despite her attempts to hold them locked tight.

The man frowned and looked off across the mesquite pasture for a while, then faced her again, scowling. "Don't make this a habit." He pulled out his wallet and handed her the money.

That scowl made her want to throw the greenbacks in his face. Instead, she took the cash and thanked him. Swallowing the bitter pill of her pride, she walked back to her truck. Then she took one look at her child, smiling with those big brown eyes, and she kicked herself for her damned pride. As long as she had food and a roof over his head, nothing else mattered.

She gritted her teeth as she headed toward her cabin. Working for Ward Ramsey was so damned hard, and she couldn't bear the thought of seeing the man again come Monday.

WARD SHOOK HIS HEAD as Jayme drove on down to her house, Dusty's little head bobbing with the conversation he carried on with his mom. What the hell was he doing with a woman and her child on the ranch? His body was still revved up from standing so close to her. Hiring her was asking for trouble. Trouble didn't belong in his life. He'd lost his mind, letting her work here. He strode into the barn to feed a little early and head on home.

He dumped pellets into a feed trough. Jayme had surprised him with the effort she put in and the quality of her work. He'd expected her to complain about the hours. Hell, he was exhausted by the end of the third day, and she'd been here nearly a week. But she didn't object, and she had worked as hard today as she did the first day.

Once he'd peeled enough hay off the round bale, he forked it into the stalls. Jayme knew what she was doing, too. She could mend fence as well as he did, had a sharp eye with cattle, and was much stronger than she looked. The woman impressed him, and he wasn't ready for that. And he sure as hell wasn't ready for the way his body responded to her.

His cell phone rang, and he answered it. "Hey, Cash. What's going on?"

"I hear you hired a new hand."

Dammit. Nothing got past his confirmed-bachelor neighbor. "Uh-huh. How'd you hear that?"

"Down at the feed store."

"Isn't anything private in this town?"

His friend laughed. "Hell no. So, tell me. What's she like?"

He leaned against a stall, his belly tense as it always was when Jayme was the subject of his thoughts. He filled Cash in on the basics, including that she had a kid. Being fair, he also mentioned that she was a good hand.

"So, how's that working out for you?"

Ward sighed. "I promised her two weeks."

SUNDAY DAWNED, AND by eight o'clock, Dusty was up and hungry. Jayme treasured these once-a-week family days with her son. Bean and cheese tacos were all they had for breakfast. Her secret to making them special was carne guisada seasoning in the beans. She'd eaten them all week, but Dusty thought they were a treat and ate his without complaint. Then they headed to Stamford after making a quick stop in town for gas.

Being Dusty, her son carried on a non-stop happy conversation on the way. Each time she glanced at his shining little face, she felt a powerful sense of wonder that this amazing little human being had come from her. She wanted to make this day a blessing for her son. It had been so long since the boy had done something fun, which was one of the things that made her feel like such a failure as a mom.

They'd brought their dirty laundry with them and would find someplace to take care of that chore while they were out, too.

By the time she got home she was broke, but she had taken her boy to MacDonald's and he'd played on the playscape, plus she had enough food to feed him for the next couple of weeks. What more could she ask for? For the first time, the burden of worrying about his care was lifted from her shoulders.

As she put the groceries away in the kitchen's small cupboards, she glanced into the living room where Dusty sat on the worn couch, eating a sliced apple and reading his book. They seldom lived where he could watch TV, and she often wondered if that gave him a social disadvantage in school.

He loved it when she read to him, so that was something they used to do a lot in the evenings. Nighttime had been too hectic for reading since moving here, and it had been hard when they were sleeping in the truck. It was definitely something Dusty missed. Thank goodness he had access to books at school now.

She sighed lazily and called out to him, "Feel like wading again this evening?"

"Yeah. I wish I had a fishing pole. Do you think Mr. Ramsey has any we could borrow?"

The boy was so hopeful that she couldn't say no, but her heart rebelled. Dreading asking the hard man for another favor, she said, "Well, I could talk to him, couldn't I?"

"I'll bet he does. Who wouldn't, with a pond like ours on their place? When can you ask him, Mom?"

"How about next time I see him?" Her teeth clenched. Oh, the things she'd do for this boy. Putting him first came with quite a cost at times.

They were out in front of the house later, tossing Dusty's baseball back and forth, when Ramsey came driving toward them from the direction of the barn.

Dusty waved like crazy, and the truck slowed.

She chewed the inside of her cheek. *Damn and double damn. The man's here.*

Her boss wore his usual frown with his elbow resting on the window ledge.

Her son skipped over to the road. "Hi, Mr. Ramsey. My mom wants to ask you something."

Want? Did he just say *want*? Oh, hell no, she didn't want.

Ramsey turned his cool gaze on her, that ruggedly handsome jaw of his clenched tight.

Clearing her throat, she walked toward the drive. Why could this ornery man make her knees turn to jelly? His sorry ass did nothing but frown at her.

She rubbed her damp palms on her jeans. "Hi, there. Dusty mentioned earlier that he wanted to fish. I was wondering, do you have a couple of fishing poles we could borrow?" The heat of embarrassment rose to her face. *Dammit.* With her lips pressed together, she tried not to scowl.

He stared out the windshield for a bit and then turned back. "I could probably scare something up. Haven't been fishing in a while. Your boy know how to fish?"

Squirming inwardly since her son tended to get attached to the men she worked with, she answered, "The foreman at the ranch I was on recently drove him out to the pond some. Dusty liked it a lot." She kicked the gravel at the edge of the road. As the only man around this ranch, there was a good chance her son would latch on to him, too. She gusted out some air. It was a disaster in the making.

Ramsey put the truck in gear and slowly picked up speed.

His face showed in the rearview mirror—handsome, dispassionate. She frowned and looked away. What went on in the man's head? And why in the hell did she feel a shiver where she shouldn't when he met her eyes in the mirror?

LATER, WHEN DINNER was almost ready, she sent Dusty in to wash his hands. The homey smell of fried potatoes and hamburger patties filled the room, but it didn't calm her. Anxiety about Blacke had kept her company while she cooked. The danger he posed, his threats, all the evil of him, had filled her thoughts. She hadn't slept much last night. Hating him, hating the thought of him, she seemed unable to banish him from her mind.

She needed to do more, but what else could she do? Was a simple phone call illegal? Should she contact the authorities, or would they think she was being paranoid? Would they even be able to do anything? Look what it took to get a restraining order. And stalking laws were a joke. Maybe since Blacke had been to prison it would be different. But what if she reported him and they gave her location away? She couldn't stop worrying about that. Right now, only one person from her past knew where she was, and her old boss would keep his mouth shut.

She dished up their plates and laid them on the table, forcing a smile as Dusty bounced into the room and sat down. "You say grace today, young man. Then we'll dig in."

A while later, as they finished eating dinner, a vehicle drove up, and soon after, a knock sounded at the door.

When she opened it, she found Ramsey facing her, and her pulse immediately sped up at the sight of the handsome man in her doorway. Why was he here?

He looked down and scuffed his boot on the step, clearly uncomfortable. When he met her gaze, he hooked his thumb over his shoulder. "I found some poles and tackle. You all want to fish tonight or what?"

"Yes! We do, don't we, Momma?" Dusty yelled from behind her.

"I guess we do." Well, this was unexpected. Maybe he wasn't such a big bad wolf after all.

Ramsey turned and headed back to his truck. She stood for a few seconds, watching his swinging stride. From behind she couldn't see his frown. He was just another sexy cowboy—and her body responded accordingly.

A few minutes later, she and Dusty stepped out the door, heading for her Chevy. She wasn't sure what to expect from her boss this evening. Glancing in his direction, she encountered his piercing stare. Crap, he was hot. It was so damned hard to reconcile the unflinching temperament of the man with his striking good looks. Skippy peered over the back of the truck and barked a hello.

Ramsey leaned his head out his window and called, "Ride with me."

Dusty sat in the center of the Ford's bench seat, bouncing up and down and all over her boss with questions about his poles, his tackle, and what kinds of fish he thought they'd catch.

She smiled and turned to her window. The early evening light softened the edges of trees and brush. Dusty hadn't been this happy in a long time. It had been worth asking her boss for the poles. What she hadn't at all anticipated was that the man would accompany them fishing.

They bumped and rolled their way down the unused dirt track, finally stopping at a large, clear space of shoreline. Lacy salt cedars lined the pond around the rest of the water's edge, and oaks and mesquite trees grew near. Dried cattle and hog tracks led up to the water, and bugs flitted across the surface.

Ramsey gestured toward the opening in the trees. "This is a nice spot to cast a line. You good at casting your line, boy?"

Dusty nodded his head energetically. Her son was so eager to please.

"Well, we'll see. I'll let you try both of my poles. Seeing as how you're the fisherman of the family, you get to pick the best one. Your momma can have the other."

Her boy grinned like a madman.

She smiled. Being called the "fisherman of the family" had made Dusty's day. How had Ramsey known that it would? Standing back, she let the boys work.

Her boss pulled down the tailgate and Skippy jumped down to the ground. Ward opened the tackle box. Picking up a flashy metal spinner with rubber bait, he showed it to Dusty. "We're going after some big old bass in this pond. We need to find just the right thing to catch them." He leaned over the box, which drew in Dusty, too, and together they examined the rest of the box's contents. Ramsey described how each item was used before giving several suggestions. When Dusty made his pick, her boss nodded his head solemnly in approval, bringing a huge grin to the boy's face.

At the edge of the pond, her boy carefully cast his bait out into the water. Then he reeled it in, the spinner tracking just below the surface as it neared him. Skippy plopped down beside him, eyeing the water with an intent gaze.

The next throw went much farther, and Ramsey said, "I think that pole's a keeper. What do you say?" He stared intently at her boy, as if his response were incredibly important.

Dusty nodded. "Oh yeah, I like this one."

Nodding solemnly, Ramsey turned to Jayme and motioned to the other pole. "All yours. Need any help?"

"Nope. Think I can handle it, but I won't guarantee I'll catch anything. Like you said, Dusty's the fisherman in the family." She quickly baited and cast her line, impressed and surprised at how Ramsey interacted with her son. He seemed completely in tune with him. And Dusty was eating it up.

The man watched every move her son made, making comments and nodding as the boy cast and reeled in his line. Dusty got a couple of bites but didn't set his hook before the wily bass got away. His shoulders slumped, and he sighed in disappointment each time.

POOR KID, HE COULDN'T catch a break. The third time Dusty lost a fish, Ward put his hand on the boy's shoulder and gave it a squeeze. "The reason the bass in this pond are so old is because they're smart. We've just got to be smarter."

Dusty smiled. "Really? You could teach me to be smarter. I listen good, and I read all sorts of books. If all you got to do is get smarter to catch them, well, they're goners."

Ward laughed—a rough and strangled sound that rasped his throat. He licked his lips, drawing his brows together. It'd been a while since he'd felt like laughing, and he obviously needed practice. The boy was a good kid, and he tried hard to learn. Something about his smile made Ward's chest ache, deep down where he hadn't felt anything in a good long while. The strange and uncomfortable feeling had been bothering him all week.

As Dusty cast his line again, Ward nodded encouragement. Teaching the boy to fish this evening felt good. With that thought came a slowly tightening knot in his gut. Getting close to the kid was a mistake. The boy didn't belong here. Ward turned his back on him and stared out over the water. Skippy came up and nudged his hand. Ward fondled his ears, taking comfort from him, as he always did.

Right at dusk, when it looked like he wouldn't catch anything, Dusty got a nibble, set the hook, and pulled up a small crappie. He grinned like crazy.

The corner of Ward's mouth twitched up. That fish might have been a five-pound bass, the boy was so proud. A dull pain settled in his chest. He pressed his lips tight before removing the fish from Dusty's line. The boy would be leaving soon. Ward threw the small fish back into the pond and grimaced. Damned if he wouldn't make sure of that.

Chapter Three

After dropping off Dusty and Jayme, Ward ate his microwave dinner and leaned back in his recliner in front of the TV, staring out the window into the night. His head ached. Though he still couldn't figure out how to fire his ranch hand, he was even more sure now that he had to let Jayme go. Time was running out. With a deep sigh, he lay his head back.

Skippy padded over from the couch and sat down by the side of Ward's chair. The dog reached out his nose and gently touched his master's hand.

"Hey, Skip." He stroked the dog's soft neck and fondled his ears.

The family room had always comforted him when he was growing up. Now it could tear him to pieces. As he stared at the mantel, he allowed memories of Elizabeth and Caleb to play out before his eyes. Ward breathed in sharply, his fists clenching.

Skippy followed him into the kitchen. These were the nights Ward didn't allow himself to drink. Feeling sorry for himself and getting drunk was not a habit he would let himself develop. And it was never a good thing to focus on his losses.

After pouring a glass of milk, he let the dog outside. Warm humidity blew in the door on the soft breeze, and crickets chirped in the darkness. It was a mild evening, one in sharp contrast to his mood.

He walked back into the living room with his drink. Television didn't appeal to him, and sleep was the last thing on his mind. The *Co-op* and *American Farmer* magazines had been read and discarded on the coffee table long ago.

His thoughts slid to Jayme and her boy and the problem they presented. What should he do? The woman was one of the best hands who'd worked with him in a long time. He liked the quiet way she worked, and she really knew her way around cattle. Plus, he never had to tell her twice about anything. Her looks worked against her, though.

Sure thing, he couldn't keep other men around when he had her with him. A gorgeous gal like her working with of a bunch of ranch hands? Not hardly. They'd never get anything done. And, come harvest, he would need to hire other hands.

He frowned. She had that letter. It seemed that things had worked out fine at that other place for two years.

To be honest, though, Jayme and her son were a distraction to him too. Without thinking, his gaze followed her while they did chores. That woman was so damned good to look at.

Jeans and a T-shirt couldn't hide her curves, and when she was walking away, her ass was something to behold. His chest tightened with the memory.

The truth was that, despite his best efforts, his body responded to hers several times a day. That was a problem. Elizabeth had died almost ten years ago, and somehow having a woman working at his side again settled a missing part of him back in place. His breath caught in his throat. That wasn't right.

And then there was Dusty. The boy needed a man. The child looked at him with hero worship in his eyes. He didn't deserve to be worshiped. He'd killed the little boy who used to feel that way about him. No way would he allow that to happen again.

The woman and her boy had to go.

Determined to break the spell, he grabbed his Stetson from the hat rack. A change of scenery was what he needed. He called Skippy in from the yard, and they loaded up in the truck.

Twenty minutes later, he wandered the aisles of Allsup's, the smell of old grease from the fried chicken they sold filling his nose. A small pack of white powdered donuts caught his eye. On a whim, he picked it up.

After paying for his purchase, he stepped out the glass door and ran into Cash. Ward shoved out his hand. "What's up, bud?"

His friend gripped his hand warmly. "Nothing but taxes. You still got that lady hand?"

"Hell, yes." Dammit. The guy knew just how to tease him and loved it.

Cash laughed. "What does she look like?"

Ward stared down at the ground and scuffed his boot. "She's all right, I guess."

"Yeah, well, you let me know how that works out." Cash grinned and slapped him on the back, then headed for his truck.

Ward walked across the parking lot, cussing himself under his breath for being such a soft touch. Half the county was probably laughing at him. Or, even worse, thought he'd hired her for more than a ranch hand. Heat rose to his face when he considered that. God, would these two weeks never end?

JAYME'S SECOND SATURDAY morning arrived. As she helped Dusty find something to wear, her stomach churned acid up her throat, burning like fire. She still had a couple of days before her two weeks were up, and she had an idea that Ramsey had a resounding *no* in mind for her staying on. His off-putting attitude hadn't changed since her first day of work. The man appeared to be marking time until he let her go. Well, damn him, she wouldn't wait to be fired.

"Dusty, would you do something for me?"

"Yeah, Mom. What?"

"Mr. Ramsey is a pretty cranky guy. I guess you kind of noticed that?"

He frowned slightly. "Well, I think he's sad."

She furrowed her brows. "Really? You think so?"

"Uh-huh. Sometimes, when he looks that way, I smile at him. He doesn't smile back. I think he's too sad."

Wow. How had she missed that one? Maybe he was different with Dusty. "Anyway, would you do me a favor and not ask Mr. Ramsey any questions? I don't want him getting mad about anything."

"Sure, Mom. He won't even know I'm there."

God, he broke her heart.

Dusty helped with feeding as they waited for her boss to arrive, but she made him stand back from the round bale while she pulled the hay off. She'd discovered a rattler nestled underneath it the day before.

Dusty picked up the loose hay and placed it in front of each of the cow pens. As he was too short to throw it over the fence, it was Jayme's job to fork it into the feed troughs inside.

As they were finishing, Ramsey drove up and honked.

She put her finger to her lips as she ushered Dusty out the barn door. Everything had to go perfectly today. She figured she had one chance to keep her place on the ranch, and Ramsey had to be in a good mood for her plan to work.

Dusty rode between Ward and his mom throughout the morning as they put out feed in the different pastures. True to his word, he kept his lips zipped tight.

At one point, Ramsey said, "You're sure quiet."

Her pulse picked up. Had he noticed something was up?

Dusty nodded and grinned. That was one thing about her little man. She never had to tell him something twice. A deep sense of pride rippled through her.

Ramsey looked away, and she unclenched her fingers. The man was just being curious.

Around noon, her boss reached into the glove box and pulled out a package of powdered donuts, handing it to her son without saying a word.

Dusty beamed all over his face. "Thanks, Mr. Ramsey," he exclaimed, breaking his silence. "These are my favorite thing in the whole world." He tore open the wrapper and popped the first donut into his mouth, smacking loudly.

A half smile played across Ramsey's lips.

She shot her boy a warning look to mind his manners, but the corner of her mouth tilted up. Her boss had actually thought of her boy while he was out running errands. In spite of herself, Jayme warmed a little toward the man.

Her heart raced when they pulled up to the barn at one-thirty. Forcing her voice to remain steady, she said, "Dusty, why don't you go on over to the truck."

He scooted across her knees and got out her side.

Steeling herself, she looked her boss dead in the eyes. "My two weeks are about up."

Ramsey blinked and lifted his brows.

She'd caught him off guard, just as she'd hoped, and she pressed on. "I'm not one to overstay my welcome, and I can't help noticing you don't want me around. I've worked my hardest and done everything you've asked, and I would like to stay on here. But if this isn't something you want to continue, then tell me now. Me and my boy will go." She hoped that her taking the initiative would convince him to let her stay. If she only had more time, she knew she could change his mind about her.

Ramsey looked away from her direct gaze and stared out the windshield for a full two minutes with narrowed eyes. His normal, grouchy expression rode his face.

She kept her mouth shut and waited him out.

He scowled, his brown eyes hard as steel. "I know damn well I'll regret this. You two can stay on. You do your work and keep out of my way. If that changes—if there comes a time when you can't do your job—then the deal's off. You're out of here."

Well, her strategy had worked, but, dammit, did he have to be such an ass? She threw him her own scowl. "You got it!" and swept out of the truck, mentally cussing his rude ass all the way back to her ride. Would it have hurt him to say something nice to her, just this once?

At least she didn't have to yank Dusty out of school. That's what had worried her most. She'd work for Ramsey, and she would give him her best, just as she would any employer. But, holy hell, screw him and the horse he rode in on. She didn't need a friend, she just needed a job so she could support her son.

WHEN SHE GOT BACK TO the house, she stopped Dusty in the living room. "Honey, do you mind if I rest by myself for a while?" She felt frayed and jangled, and her son didn't need to bear the brunt of her raw nerves.

Dusty stared, his brows drawn together, for a few seconds. "Sure, Mom." He grabbed his book off the coffee table and sat down to read.

Though she was relieved as hell to have a permanent job, her nose was still way out of joint at the way that damn Ramsey had given it to her. Did he need to be so damn rude and surly all the time?

Lying down, she punched her fist into the mattress and continued to simmer. She wished she could throw the freaking job in his face for the way he treated her. But she had Dusty to consider, and his needs came first, always, no matter what it cost her financially or emotionally. That little boy out there was counting on her to show up at the barn Monday morning, no matter how hard facing Ramsey again would be.

She gritted her teeth as her simmer hit a full rolling boil. She was so damn mad and, if she was brutally honest with herself, hurt. She squeezed her fists until her nails bit into her palms, then, turning onto her side, she curled into a ball, wrapping her arms around her knees. Silent tears leaked onto the pillow. She burrowed her face into it, hiding from the light. How could she go on?

Her limbs weighed her down. Each labored breath was one too many. It took everything she had to scratch out a living for her son. She couldn't live in fear of Blacke anymore, peering over her shoulder night and day. Uncurling, she wiped her face and pulled a second pillow tight into her belly. A small voice inside her said it all. She couldn't face her life alone.

She woke, bleary-eyed and drained of energy. Turning over, her gaze fell on Dusty's picture. He was her compass, the thing that kept her true. As long as she had him, she could go on. She slid on her jeans and boots and went to find her son.

WARD, SITTING BY HIMSELF in the quiet house, tilted his head back and groaned. He'd had every intention of letting the woman go, and with some kind of answer prepared, he could have done it. But she'd caught him off guard and his mind had frozen.

Jayme was fierce and yet so vulnerable. Truth be told, he might never have fired her. She was a strong and reliable worker, and he admired her spirit. He hadn't made things easy for her, and she had stuck it out without complaint.

Then there was the boy. If he made her leave, Dusty would have to switch schools again. Lord know how much he had already missed. Constant change wasn't good for a kid. Even he knew that. He couldn't do that to the him.

He gripped the arms of his chair, wondering how the hell to face the consequences of his decision. How could he handle working with the woman every day? And what about the way the boy made him feel? He hadn't felt this emotional since the first couple of years after the accident. He didn't like it one bit.

Chapter Four

Jayme inhaled deeply. Early morning was a wonderful time of day. The sun was mild, and the slightly damp air was free of the dust that would fill her nostrils later in the afternoon. She peeled off more hay from the round bale in the barn. If only she didn't have to face Ramsey in a little while. The man might despise her, but she would make damn sure he had every reason to respect her.

The morning went about as she expected. Her boss had nothing to say to her, simply jerking his thumb over his shoulder at the truck when it came time to check the fencing. They drove in silence until lunch, unless he needed to order her around. It proved to be more of the same in the afternoon, right up to when he dropped her at the barn to burn trash and other fun chores.

She put the last of the feed sacks in the burn barrel and studied the lacy pieces of char riding the heated wind rising from the fire. The man hadn't said one extra word to her all day. Hell, he'd barely looked at her. What was his problem? Whatever it was, she needed to figure it out—and pretty damn quick if she wanted to keep Dusty in school. That was what really mattered.

Closing her eyes, she blew out a long sigh. She'd never dreamed it would be so difficult working for a man who didn't like her. It really bothered her, and she hadn't expected that. With no friends because of the transient nature of her job and no lover, having a boss who approved of her was the only real positive in her life—besides Dusty, of course. The lack of appreciation she felt in this job left a hole, and it was getting harder and harder to keep going.

That evening, as she was pouring cow cubes into the last pen, Ramsey walked in. Peering over the bars, he stared intently at the heifer, which was due to calve, then grunted and walked back out of the barn, flicking a wave at Dusty on his way.

She scowled at his receding back. Damn the man. He should have said hello or something...anything. But no, not him. Not bad-ass Ramsey. It hurt more than she expected. More than she wanted it to.

Her son was silent, watching her. For once he didn't say hi to her boss, only returned his wave. "Momma, you don't like him much, do you?"

"I don't think he's a very nice man."

Dusty drew a circle in the dust with his boot. "If I was sad, I wouldn't act nice either."

There he went, standing up for the man again. Her son wanted to like Ramsey so bad he had blinders on.

After they got home, she fixed a quick dinner while Dusty took his bath. Even at eight, her boy still enjoyed playing in the bathtub. Though she didn't have real bath toys, she gave him cups and bowls, and he sang as he poured water and splashed. Somehow, his delight in what little they had only made her feel more like a failure.

If she'd ever stayed in one place, maybe she could have accumulated more things to make a better home for him. Once, her dad had asked her why she didn't work on the ranch he managed. But working for that man wouldn't make for a happy home. Her stern, distant father had nothing to offer her.

Dusty read a book to her and she helped him say his prayers before tucking him into their bed.

She stepped out the front door and checked for snakes before sitting down on the steps. A breeze blew across her face and, this far out in the country, every star shone bright in the deep, dark sky. Nights like this made her realize her problems were tiny in comparison. Self-pity was pretty hard with all that majesty overhead.

She leaned back against the door and closed her eyes. Counting her blessings one by one took a while. Weeks had passed since her last tally, which might be why her mood was so stinky nowadays. Without counting her blessings, she could start feeling sorry for herself—even blame others for her pain.

Dusty's worried expression when he'd asked if she liked Ramsey had stuck with her. Dammit, she was a jerk for telling her boy that the man wasn't nice. Dusty wanted a man to look up to and, unfortunately, her boss was the only one around.

It was her fault her boy didn't have a man in his life. She couldn't find her way to trusting men – though she'd tried. She dated a few guys. Once she even saw the same guy three times. But, when it came time for the rubber to meet the road, she didn't feel right. He didn't feel right. Nothing at *all* felt right. And that was the end of that. She didn't even blame the man for dumping her. That had been the last time she'd dated anyone.

She pulled her elastic out of her hair, letting it fall free on her shoulders. Rubbing her scalp, she made up her mind. Tomorrow, for her son's sake, so he could feel okay about liking her boss, she'd swallow her pride and be more understanding of that jackass Ramsey. She didn't look forward to it one damn bit.

A SCREAM PIERCED THE air. She jerked straight up in bed, eyes wide, heart battering her breastbone, looking everywhere for the danger. After a second, she realized her own voice had awakened her. Again. *Shit.*

Dusty sat halfway up. "Momma?"

"Go back to sleep, honey." She kissed him on his forehead.

He turned over and fell instantly asleep. As on so many other nights, he wouldn't remember anything about it in the morning.

It was the same damn nightmare. No matter how much she talked her way through it, the freaking thing still came back.

She got up and poured herself a glass of cold water from the fridge, then took it to the old couch, her hands still trembly and weak. A little light from the moon came in the window, coating the room a soft charcoal gray. She covered herself in her mother's quilt, soaking up its loving comfort.

One rule she didn't break was that she never dated guys on the ranches where she worked. Blacke had been one of her bosses, and the man had taken a dislike to her as soon as he realized that his clumsy advances wouldn't be returned.

The jerk had gone out of his way to make her life miserable. None of the other cowboys appreciated the crap he gave her, either, but as senior hand, just under the foreman, he got away with a lot. He took full advantage of stretching the rules, and it was one reason his rustling had slipped under the radar for so long.

She'd become suspicious when some cattle went missing from one of the herds, but given the way Blacke treated her, she'd kept her mouth shut. Not until she had gathered more evidence and could prove his involvement in the theft did she make her call to the authorities.

Blacke had overheard her.

Her nightmare was a reminder. The man was coming. It was only a matter of time until he found her, and she had to come up with some way to handle him.

SATURDAY CAME AGAIN, and Jayme looked forward to an outing with Dusty after work. She was taking him to the donut shop, where they planned to eat their fill. Now that she had a steady job, this was the first of many more fun things she hoped to do with Dusty. She ruffled her son's hair as he rode next to her. He was such a good boy. *This is what being a good mom feels like.*

When they walked into the store, Noreen greeted them like friends.

Dusty rushed over to the counter. "Miss Noreen, guess what? We're living at Mr. Ramsey's ranch, and I go to school, and there's a pond right behind my house, and I've caught fish all by myself!"

Jayme smiled. In some ways her son was mature beyond his years, and in others he was still so young and innocent. She loved him so much sometimes, it felt like her heart would burst.

Tipping her hat to Noreen, she breathed deep, filling her nose with the wonderful smells of coffee and warm donuts. "We'd each like three of those scrumptious things." She pointed at the glazed creations under the counter. "And I'd like a cup of coffee. Do you have milk for my little man here?"

Noreen smiled. "I reckon I can scare up some for this big strong boy. So Ramsey had a spot for you, huh?"

Turning her head so that Dusty wouldn't notice, Jayme rolled her eyes. "Oh yeah, he gave me a two-week trial period and then graciously allowed me to stay." *And the man still isn't happy about it. I wish to hell I knew why he dislikes me so much.*

Noreen laughed and shook her head as she grasped the donuts with her tongs. "Well, good luck, honey. You'll need it. He hasn't always been such an ass, though." She handed the bag of donuts to Jayme and then turned to pour her coffee. "Ward lost his wife and little boy in a car wreck. The child was about four. The man hasn't been fit to work for since." Setting the cup of coffee on the counter, she went to the back for Dusty's milk.

Dusty looked at his mom. "I told you. He's sad."

Jayme ruffled his hair and grimaced. "Yeah, you did. I need to listen to you more often, don't I, Mr. Smarty-Pants?"

He giggled and looked down, scuffing the toe of his boot on the hardwood floor.

She bit her lip and stared at her own boots. It seemed that Ramsey had his own share of grief. She hadn't seen that coming; she'd just seen him acting mad all the time. She'd never seen his sadness like Dusty had.

Noreen came back and handed the milk over the counter to Jayme.

Jayme reached for it. "Well, I'm sure we'll see you again soon, since donuts are Dusty's favorite food."

Noreen waved and walked toward the back of the store. "Bye now."

Jayme stepped into her truck, for the first time feeling empathy for Ramsey and his hard ways. Maybe she should have been cutting him a little more slack. She almost—*almost*—felt like a jackass.

What kind of person would she be if she lost Dusty? Would she be an asshole too? How could she go on living with her son gone? Little fingers of nausea tickled her stomach.

Despite how hard the bastard was on her, he had some slack coming from now on. She would imagine herself losing Dusty before she reacted.

THE NEXT SATURDAY AFTERNOON, Ward stood at the barn door as Jayme and Dusty drove on out toward their little house. Damn, when he was around her, he couldn't wait to get away. How could he work with her when his heart pounded, his breath caught in his throat, and parts of him he didn't want noticed came to attention?

Being around her was only bearable when the boy was literally sitting between them. Ward batted a fly away from his ear. Now, that Dusty was a smart kid. Ward had to hand it to Jayme, the woman did a great job raising him. He was mannerly, quiet—well, mostly quiet—and he knew how to behave around the stock. No, Ward didn't have any complaints about her son.

The problem was Jayme. It was like being buzzed by bees when she was around. And it wasn't that she dressed inappropriately or tried to attract his attention; it was just that no matter how hard he resisted, his gaze strayed to her firm breasts or her slender waist. Just the other day, he had had to hold a hay bale in front of his crotch to keep from advertising his attraction. Dammit, he didn't want that hot body of hers bending and moving while they did chores. Being attracted to her was wrong. His selfishness had cost him his wife. And he sure wouldn't go through that kind of loss again.

He slapped his hat against his thigh. There had to be a way to change how Jayme affected him. With a frown, he climbed into his truck and drove back to the house to take a shower.

Casey and Annie had asked him over for barbeque this afternoon. If anyone could pull him away from the ranch, it was his best friend. The two of them had gotten into so much hell in high school and rodeo college that they'd finally quit telling Annie the stories. She'd been ready to whup them both.

He enjoyed accepting their invitations once in a while, however, just to get out of the house.

Casey had a beautiful family, and that family was what made it hard to go over there. Kylie, at fourteen, was a young lady now, while ten-year-old David looked just like his daddy had at that age. Ward didn't feel jealous, but their happy family life knifed straight into the heart of his loss.

He stopped in town and bought a twelve-pack of beer before driving on over to visit. Jayme's face flitted before his eyes. Maybe his best friend could help him sort things out. As he pulled up in front of the long, rock ranch house, Casey's wife, Annie, came out to welcome him.

"Come in here, you handsome thing," she shouted from the porch. "Casey's out back at the pit, and dinner's in a half-hour."

She raised her arms, ready to give him a hug and a kiss on the cheek as he walked up.

The woman was a tiny thing, and he had to bend way down. Her tight hug eased some of his tension.

Annie let him go and pushed him toward the open door. "Get on back there and keep that man out of my hair."

Grinning, he walked into the house, smelling cornbread cooking as he wound his way through the rustic den and homey kitchen to the back screen door.

Casey looked up from the barbeque pit and waved. "Come over here and help me with this thing. Thanks for bringing the beer. Put it in the ice chest over there." He nodded at the red-and-white cooler near the picnic table under the oak tree.

Ward looked around the newly mown yard. "Where are the kids?"

"They both spent the night with friends. They should be here in a little while. We told them dinner was at three."

Casey tilted his head, looking Ward over from head to toe as he flipped the sausages and steaks over with his fork. A spicy aroma filled the air. "So I hear you hired a new hand."

Ward grimaced. *Great, people are already gossiping.* "How did you find out?"

"You know nothing's a secret in this town."

"Yeah, I hired one. Didn't plan on it. I said yes before I could say no, I guess. It's a woman, a single mom." *And she's gorgeous, Lord help me.*

Casey raised his brows and nudged the cooking meat with his fork. "How did that happen?"

"Last guy I had booked out of there last month, leaving the place trashed. She came with references and, hell, she seemed desperate. But, shit, I never would have done it if I knew she had a boy. She didn't let on about that until after I said yes."

Casey shook his head and hung the fork on the hook at the front of the grill. "You're good with kids. Is it really a problem? Does he misbehave or something?"

Ward rubbed the back of his neck. "No, he's a good kid. But women can't be good ranch hands. And her kid's going to be a distraction. You know that."

Casey peered through narrowed eyes. "I don't agree. Seems to me she's got a reason to be a good hand, and that's her boy. You might just have a hand that stays a while even though you're an asshole to work for, my friend."

Yeah, yeah, everybody knows I'm an asshole. Ward crossed his arms. Casey didn't get it. "I said she had two weeks. Then the next thing I know she's asking me if I'm going to send her packing, and, like an idiot, I let her stay. A woman and a kid are nothing but trouble. You wait and see." How could his friend not see the problem? Of course having a woman around wasn't going to work. He should know that.

Casey glanced his way while he wiped his hands on his apron. "Maybe that boy needs you. You've got a lot you could give him." He picked up the fork and pointed it at Ward. "He's got a momma and no daddy around. He needs a man in his life. You said he's good, and you could make him better. Think on that." Casey moved a couple of steaks, closed the lid on the grill, and walked over and pulled two beers out of the cooler.

He handed one to Ward. "What's her name?"

"Jayme Bonner." This conversation was *not* going the way he'd hoped. Shit, Casey should have his back. And spend more time with the boy? After the way the kid affected him? Hell, no. It would mean more time with her, too. Out of the question.

Casey nodded. "Does she do her work?"

"And then some." She was a damn good worker. That's what made this whole thing so hard.

"Well, there you go. She's a hard worker, and she's got a reason to stay. I don't see the problem, buddy."

Ward scowled and took a drink of his beer. Damn the woman. Why did she have to look so good in a pair of Wranglers? "I can't put my finger on it. I just don't like it."

"Hell, you spend so much time being an angry asshole that when something good comes along, it feels like a kick in the butt."

Tipping his hat, Ward laughed. "Thanks. That's some analogy, partner."

Casey slapped him on the back. "Get over it. Take it easy and relax around her. Get to know her. She won't bite. I'm sure she could use some human kindness after a few weeks of putting up with your sorry ass."

Ward left not long after dark. On the drive home, he considered Casey's suggestions. Maybe the way to lessen Jayme's effect on him was to learn a little about her. No more mystery woman; just an everyday ranch hand. He had to do something. The knot in his stomach was becoming permanent. But how could he talk to the woman? She didn't like him one damn bit.

He checked his rearview mirror and sighed. Maybe there was something to what Casey had said about the boy too. He probably could use a father figure in his life. But could Ward handle getting closer to another child? His heart wrenched as he remembered the boy's smile—the way Dusty's eyes had begun to worship him. If spending time with the boy was this hard, he didn't want to do it. Couldn't do it. He'd had enough of that gut-wrenching feeling after his loss ten years ago. He couldn't lose another child.

Chapter Five

Saturday night, Jayme read to her son in their lumpy bed until he fell asleep. As she stroked his soft curls, she tried to untangle the puzzle Ramsey posed. Why did her boss dislike her so much? The man barely spoke to her, avoided looking her in the face, and stayed as far away from her as the job allowed. She needed this job—it had to work out—but she didn't know what to do to change the damn man's mind.

He was an enigma. Uncertain why he'd let her stay, she was clueless how to make him appreciate her. She always did a good job. She was proactive and paid great attention to detail, and caught illness and injury in the cattle before they had a chance to get bad. Yet still the man's disapproval was apparent. He made it obvious he couldn't stand to be around her. What was she doing wrong? Somehow she had to fix it.

After lunch the next day, she took Dusty over to the ranch house and borrowed a lawnmower and a string trimmer. She and Dusty had decided it was time they made their little house look more like a home.

After helping her load the mower into the back of her truck, Ramsey walked over to Dusty's window. "How about fishing with me this evening?"

The boy's face lit up like a star. "Sure! At our tank?"

"Yep. We need to teach those fish over there a lesson. I'll be by about 6:30, if that's all right with you?" He looked at Jayme.

Brows raised, she nodded. "Sure. We'll be ready." How about that? Another fishing invitation from tough guy. As she drove off, she glanced in her rearview mirror.

Ramsey stood there, watching them drive away.

What was the man thinking? Would she ever figure him out?

Dusty hung his head out the window, waving at Ramsey and bouncing up and down on his knees on the seat. He promised to help her with the yard so they would finish in time to fish.

After two hours of hot, sweaty work, the newly mowed and trimmed lawn made their cabin more like a real home. The sight eased something inside her. Maybe things would work out here. Then she remembered the phone call. She and Dusty weren't safe as long as that monster was on her trail.

DUSTY HAD BEEN MONITORING the time. When she came out of the bathroom, he reminded her, "We've got ten minutes, Mom. Hurry up and finish getting dressed."

"Okay, buster. I guess I won't put on my makeup or roll my hair, huh?"

He scrunched his face up for a second and then grinned. "Right. You never wear makeup or roll your hair."

"And a lucky girl I am, I say." She'd been a tomboy all her life, and though she knew how to do those things, she seldom did.

A few minutes later, Ramsey drove up out front. Dusty jumped from the couch. "Come on, Mom. He's here."

After packing several bottles of water and an ice pack into a cooler, she went out the door after her excited little guy. Her boss had a half smile on his face—until he looked up at her and dropped it. *Jerk. Wait, um, never mind.* Ugh. This wasn't going to be easy.

"Hurry. Mr. Ramsey said the fish should start biting any time now."

Tucking the poles and tackle box in the tidy back of the truck along with Skippy, she grumped, "I'm in, I'm in."

They bumped their way down to the same place as before. Ramsey pulled down the tailgate and opened the tackle box so that he and Dusty could sort out their gear.

Jayme's gaze was irresistibly drawn to Ramsey's rippling forearms and the way his shirt hugged his broad back. And, oh Lord, the man had the most beautiful mouth. She was all but salivating over the guy. Her throat constricted as she swallowed.

Ramsey caught her gaze and nodded to her, mumbling, "You can call me Ward."

Her jaw dropped as she gave him a wide-eyed stare. Was he actually being nice to her? Holy shit.

He turned to her boy. "That's still Mr. Ramsey to you, buddy."

Dusty laughed. "Well, I know that."

"Just making sure." Ruffling Dusty's hair, Ward rested his hand on the boy's slim shoulder. "You need to get some meat on your bones, kid."

"Mom always says that. I eat a lot, but I think my belly takes it all, and it doesn't share."

Ramsey—Ward—laughed his strange, strangled laugh. "Well, that won't last long. You're due to fill out." He patted Dusty and walked to the edge of the muddy bank.

Tears burned behind her eyes at the hero worship on Dusty's face. Even if she was the best mom on the planet, she couldn't make up for the lack of a man in his life. All one had to do was look at him twice, and her son was his for the asking.

How could she protect him? These men were short-term, and each time she and Dusty left one behind, Dusty's hurt grew a little deeper. How could she keep him from giving his heart away? She grabbed her pole and walked a little way down the bank, tossing her line out into the water and reeling furiously.

Her son cast and reeled into the glassy surface of the pond with Ward encouraging him and offering advice.

The boy hung on every word, his face one big smile.

Jayme watched as Ward knelt at Dusty's feet, checking his bait after it got caught on something under the water. His broad shoulders stretched the seams of his denim shirt.

Her gaze wandered down to his trim waist and the muscular, denim-encased butt resting on his bootheel. A warm wave of attraction flushed through her. She frowned. This reaction was no good.

As if sensing her, Ward glanced over his shoulder as he stood up.

Caught, she turned and launched her line into the water, then reeled it in. The last thing she needed was her boss thinking she had a crush on him. What a humiliation that would be.

Soon Dusty got a nibble, and Ward talked him through setting the hook. Her son landed a good-sized bass and jumped up and down on the bank, yelling for her to come see.

She walked over and hugged Dusty's shoulder as Ward slipped the fish onto the stringer. Those hips of his. Why did the man have to look so sexy today? "That's a big one, honey," she praised her son.

"Do you think we have enough for a fish fry now?" Dusty asked.

"Not yet, but we're getting there." She handed her pole to her boss. "Why don't you take this and try your luck? He's got his heart set on a fish fry, and I never add anything to the pot."

The man's sharp glance sent blood rushing through her veins, and she felt the heat of a blush rising to her face. Dammit, this was ridiculous. She was a grown woman, not some schoolgirl. She should be able to control her reaction to the guy.

Ward nodded at her son. "Buddy, it's you and me now. Let's catch us some fish."

Dusty grinned. "Yeah, let's catch some fish."

From her seat safely far away on the tailgate, it was easy to enjoy her boy's happiness. She swung her legs back and forth, lulled by the sounds of the bugs and birds living around the water. Skippy came up and nosed her hand, eager to be petted.

What was going on with her? She was so seldom attracted to men these days; how could she be drawn to a guy who couldn't stand the sight of her? Maybe that was his appeal. Because he didn't like her, there was no chance of getting involved with him. Appalled, she bit her lip and turned away from the pond. The whole thing was crazy.

Ram—Ward's—fishing invitation had surprised her, and the attention he was showing Dusty tonight was heartwarming. Okay, maybe he was a little less of a jerk than she had thought.

Her son let out a yelp, and she turned her head to see what was going on.

Ward reeled in something heavy on his line.

The boy grabbed the net and leaned way out over the water as the fish got closer.

Jayme lurched off the tailgate and ran over to them, grabbing the back of Dusty's pants as he used both hands to scoop a large bass out of the pond.

"Your fish is bigger than mine, Mr. Ramsey!"

Ward bent and pulled the hook out of the fish's mouth before adding him to the stringer. "Your turn, Dusty. Let's see another big one on your line now."

"Yeah!"

Her boy was nearly beside himself with joy, and she owed it all to this strange man standing beside her. He was like Dr. Jekyll and Mr. Hyde—first cold and hard, then kind like this. What was she supposed to think? Who was he really?

Ward and Dusty cast out at different angles and reeled in their lines. By late evening, the stringer held three more bass. Jayme cleaned them, and by the time they knocked off for the night, she had fillets in two ziplock bags. They definitely had enough for a little fish fry. Dusty was so excited he could hardly stand still.

Jayme remembered her new resolution and the fact that she wanted to change Ward's mind about her. Holding up the bags of fish, she nodded at Ramsey. "Mr.... Uh, Ward, will you join us for a fish fry next Saturday afternoon? You helped catch them, so you should help us eat them." Her pulse sped up in anticipation of his answer.

Dusty's imploring look would have melted the hardest heart.

Ward stared out at the water a long moment, then looked down at her son. "Well, I've waited a long time to catch those old boys. We'd better try them and see if they taste any good."

Dusty threw his arms around Ward's waist and hugged him.

Ward jerked and blinked, then swallowed hard and shifted his weight from foot to foot.

Shit fire! She clenched her jaws, her lips jammed together in a thin line.

Eventually, the man pulled her boy close and patted his back.

She loosened her fists. Ramsey had better be glad he finally hugged Dusty back. There was no excuse for him taking so long. What if he hadn't? It would've killed Dusty. She'd been a fool to think the man cared about her son. Turning on her heel, she strode to the truck before Dusty could see her face.

When the boy got to her, she held the door for him and kept her face averted until they got back to the house. Her son yelled goodbye to Ramsey as he drove off, and she held her mouth shut. *Asshole.* And she meant it.

WARD SAT IN THE LIVING room in his recliner long after dinner and dark. The usual silence surrounded him. Perhaps sensing Ward's troubles, Skippy lay next to his chair instead of over on the couch. Ward's head was in turmoil, his heart beating slow and heavy in his chest. This evening's fishing at the tank had undone him. He couldn't figure out how or why, but it had.

That boy was a great kid—and a good little fisherman too. He listened to everything Ward told him and had the ability to put it to use. That was the mark of intelligence.

Ward hadn't been prepared for the boy to hug him, though. Dusty was so thin, so vulnerable. Ward's heart ached when he'd felt Dusty's small shoulders.

Jayme had been ready to wring Ward's neck while he stood there like an idiot, and he didn't blame her. Who wouldn't want a hug from a super kid like that?

Ward had planned to get to know the woman a little better during their fishing session tonight, but that sexy body of hers had distracted him too much.

Jayme was a tough one, and she didn't like him one bit. It was his own fault, he knew that. He didn't treat her right. He was a bastard, and he didn't know how to be anything else.

But that boy, now. It was obvious that boy had needs. Maybe Ward was man enough to do something about that.

THE NEXT MORNING, WARD arrived at the barn as soon as Jayme got back from dropping Dusty off at his bus. With his new resolve in mind, he walked over and leaned on a stall. "Morning. We've gotten a jump on a lot that needed doing these past few weeks. So we'll be working things a bit different, beginning today. That boy's of an age where he needs more help with his homework and such. We'll start knocking off at five in the evenings."

Jayme's mouth fell open.

He smothered a laugh and grinned lopsidedly. "Not what you expected me to say. I'm an asshole. I know it, and so does everybody else, apparently. But that boy never makes a fuss, no matter how long you work. Maybe now *he'll* have a little more time for fun." Ward pivoted on his heel and walked toward the barn door.

Jayme found her voice. "Thanks," she called after him.

Without looking back, he nodded and raised his hand. His lips twitched into a smile and he stuck his hands in his pockets. Who said you couldn't teach an old dog new tricks?

THE WEEK PASSED QUICKLY for Jayme. Coming home early made everything so much easier. With her help, Dusty finished the papers he couldn't do alone, and his catch-up homework from starting the end-of-year school term late was finally done.

After work on Friday, she picked up a couple of things at the grocery store that she needed for the fish fry. By Saturday afternoon, it was all she could do to keep Dusty still. In truth, she was jittery herself—nervous as hell at the prospect of having her boss over for dinner. How in the hell would she talk to the guy? They'd never had a conversation before.

She'd told Ward to stop by around six, and she remembered her new resolution. The man had been living with a terrible loss, and she was determined to put the hugging episode aside before he got to the house.

Later that afternoon, Dusty's stomach growled loudly as he stood next to her, watching her push the fillets down evenly in the skillet. The oil popped and crackled, and the smell of fish and potatoes frying filled the room. "How long before we eat, Momma?"

"Well, we sure can't do that before our guest arrives, can we?" Her stomach did a flip-flop as she pictured her boss sitting in her kitchen. But was it excitement or anxiety? Damn, he was a good-looking man.

"Yeah, but how soon until he gets here?"

She pulled her phone out of her back pocket and checked. "In about fifteen minutes, if he's on time." She reached over and turned on the burner under the corn. The potatoes were almost done. The table was set, and all she had to do was put the tea out.

Dusty went into the living room, presumably to check out the window for Ward's truck again. She flipped the fried potatoes for the last time, turning off the flame underneath them. How should she act tonight? Should she be extra friendly—try to butter him up, break through that wall he kept around himself? She made a face. No way. She couldn't stomach doing that. How could she get him to open up, though? She wanted a better relationship with him. They were so uncomfortable with each other. Something had to change. Well, they said food was the way to a man's heart. Maybe her fried fish would do the trick.

Wiping her hands on the dish towel slung over her shoulder, she pulled the iced tea out of the fridge, placing it in the center of the table next to the ketchup and salt and pepper.

A door slammed, and Dusty yelled, "He's here, Mom. Mr. Ramsey's here."

The front door opened and the steps thumped as her son raced outside, so eager for that male attention.

Her heart started to pound. She wiped her shaking hands again and headed for the living room.

At the front door, she called out to Ward. "Come on in. I'll make you a glass of iced tea." Her gaze traveled up and down the length of him, absorbing every tiny detail of his perfect physique. Blood shot to all the important parts of her body, including those not touched by a man in ages. Heat rushed to her face, and she spun around. Was this how she was going to respond to him all night? God help her.

Returning to the kitchen, she turned the fish before taking a glass from the table and filling it with ice from a tray in the freezer. After pouring it full of sweet tea, she handed it to Ward, who'd come into the room.

The man overwhelmed the small space with his broad shoulders, filling it with electric energy. He stared at her with eyes that melted her insides like the hot desert sun.

Tonight was the first time she'd seen him all cleaned up. He smelled wonderful too. Little tingles slithered around in her tummy. Dammit, why did he always affect her this way?

Dusty was standing by his side, as near as he could get to him.

Ward took the glass. "Thanks." He gazed around at the room. "This sure is different from the last time I saw it. You worked hard cleaning it up."

She pursed her lips at his words, glad to have the heat from his gaze turned elsewhere. Pulling the fillets out of the oil, she slid four more into the skillet.

Facing him again, she crossed her arms. "I believe that's the first nice thing you've ever said to me." She was surprised at how good the compliment felt.

Ward tucked his hands in his pockets and looked at his boots. "I told you I was an ass—" He glanced at Dusty.

She said, "Huh," and swept Dusty's curls out of his eyes. "Washed your hands yet, mister?"

"No, Mom." He turned and trotted off to the bathroom.

"Pick a chair, Asshole, and I'll bring you a plate." A knot of tension eased in her belly as she teased her boss.

Ward grinned and sat down.

Once his plate was filled with several fillets, lots of corn, and a pile of fried potatoes, she set it in front of him.

"This looks tasty, Jayme."

She grinned wryly at him. "My, my, we're having all sorts of firsts tonight. You've never called me by my name before." She couldn't help it. She wanted to gig him for the way he'd been treating her and, tonight, it felt safe to do that.

Ward cleared his throat and studied his food.

Dusty trotted back into the kitchen, and she laid his full plate down.

As she filled hers, she pointed to her son. "You say grace as soon as I sit down, young man." This was for Ward's benefit, so he would know they set a proper table.

Putting her plate down, she sat and scooted her chair forward, bowing her head.

Dusty reached out for Ward's hand as Jayme gave her son hers. Ward swallowed hard and inched his other hand toward the one she shoved in his direction.

The boy closed his eyes and began. "Dear God, thank you for this food. I really like fish. And I like not being hungry too. Love you, God. Amen."

She exhaled in shock. Lord, her boy had gone hungry. Shame lashed her, and she wanted to run to the bedroom and bawl her eyes out. Dammit, why did she invite Asshole to dinner, anyway? Wiping her eyes, she got rid of her tears and squeezed Dusty's shoulder. "Thanks, son. I liked your prayer."

Dusty grabbed the ketchup and squirted some on his potatoes. "Mom, I wish we had fried potatoes every night."

"I love them too." She couldn't bring herself to look at her boss.

"Do you like fried potatoes, Mr. Ramsey?" Dusty asked.

Ward nodded. "I surely do. Been a while, though."

Her son took a big bite and chewed while he talked. "You need to come eat with us more, then, 'cause Mom usually makes fried potatoes unless we have sandwiches."

Ward kept his eyes averted. "Huh."

She tapped her fork on her plate. "Keep that mouth closed while you chew, young man." As to future dinner invitations, she kept her trap shut.

After they'd eaten every speck of food, Dusty stood from the table. "Do you like to throw balls, Mr. Ramsey?"

Ward's eyebrows rose.

"I'm just saying, 'cause if you did, we could head outside and throw my baseball for a while."

Ward tilted his head. "Well, I suppose if you took it easy on me I'd figure it out. It's been a long time since I threw a ball."

"Sure, I'll throw slow until you get better. I'll take it real easy on you, like I do with Mom."

She grimaced. "Oh, really?" Since when did her son need to make allowances for her?

"Yeah. I can throw harder, but I don't want to hurt you."

Ward stood. "Sounds like you all need some mitts."

"I just throw it slow, and we still have fun." Dusty trotted back into the bedroom to get his ball.

So her boss was ready to play ball with her son, huh? Would the sun rise in the west tomorrow? She shook her head. "I just thought he wasn't very good at throwing. That kid."

As the boys tossed the ball back and forth, her hair tickled her cheek in the evening breeze. True to his word, Dusty could throw much faster and harder than she'd seen him do before. That boy was just chock-full of surprises.

Ward walked over to him a couple of times, correcting his posture and positioning his hands.

Dusty ate it up, all but shivering with delight.

Her boss was relaxed for the first time. His smile, when he talked to her son, was warm and happy. He even let the smile ride when he turned her way, and it warmed her all the way to her toes.

Closing her eyes, she tilted her head back, listening to them talk and tease each other. Her boy needed things like this. It pained her to know how much he missed out on in life, not having a father. But his real father was something he could never have.

She'd told Dusty that she fell in love with a bull rider who didn't want to be tied down with a wife and baby. She wouldn't tell him the cowboy's name because, "You're my boy—nobody else's."

In reality, Dusty's father was her secret. Nobody knew who he was, and she had no plans to change that. She was mother, father, breadwinner, and hurt doctor—everything to her boy. And that was just fine with her.

Watching Ward and Dusty play, tossing the ball back and forth, softened her heart even more toward her boss. If she wasn't careful, she might actually start to like the guy.

She got up and dusted her backside off. It was time Dusty had his bath.

Ward noticed and held onto the ball, walking over near the wooden steps. "Guess I'd better be getting on home. Thanks for a mighty nice dinner."

"Welcome." She found that she was glad her boss had come over. He'd shown a different side of himself tonight, and maybe some of that hard shell had cracked. She hoped so, anyway.

Dusty walked up. "Mr. Ramsey, do you have to go?"

"Yeah—"

Before he could say anymore, Dusty wrapped his arms around Ward's waist and hugged him hard.

Ward knelt and hugged him back.

The man must have learned his lesson the first time.

Ward held Dusty's shoulders. "Hey, I'll probably see you around tomorrow. Want to ride with me while I feed my pasture out off Highway 6?" He looked at Jayme.

She stared back. "We'll both go."

Chapter Six

Ward drove slowly back to the ranch house. The little cabin had really changed. With the yard mowed, the place looked like a proper little home. All it had needed was some care and attention.

He couldn't remember when he'd last eaten a good fish fry. Or, before Jayme and Dusty moved in, been fishing. His life had stopped years ago, and he hadn't even realized it.

What a shame Dusty didn't have a mitt for that ball. It was difficult to play without one. The boy had a nice little arm on him, too.

Damn, that woman was tough, though. Tough as rawhide. Being called out was rough, but he knew he deserved it. He'd ridden her hard the past few weeks—way harder than any hand he ever hired—and she'd taken it and come to work the next day ready for more.

So, yeah, he was an asshole. But he wanted to be different in the way he treated her, and he wanted to make a difference in her and Dusty's lives. The new hours were a fine start.

With her hair down, for the first time, she'd appeared softer, and—he swallowed—more beautiful. There had been something surprisingly sexy about her bare feet flitting back and forth across the kitchen floor. His eyes had tracked her sweet, rounded backside all around the room, though he'd been careful she didn't catch him.

Damn, she was sarcastic, though. He wondered what her lips would be like in a real smile, but he was the last person who'd find out. The woman obviously detested him. As for letting her boy go off alone with him? Not hardly. Good for her, though. A boy Dusty's age needed lots of looking after.

He pulled up in front of the ranch house and parked. For the first time in a long while, he dreaded entering the empty house. He didn't usually feel lonely. To be honest, about the only thing he could remember feeling was tired and angry. It was easy to feel angry. It came quickly, and he felt a certain satisfaction in getting mad. Why the hell was that? It'd been that way since...since they died.

Shoving his truck door open, he stomped his boots down on the driveway and then strode toward the front door. No matter how much he wished he'd died with them that night, he was still here—alone.

AFTER HER BOSS LEFT, Jayme sent Dusty off to start his bath while she cleaned up the kitchen. As she started on the pans, her phone rang. Pulling it out of her pocket, she gasped, flinging it away from her and across the floor. *Blacke!* It rang again. The trembling began in her knees and moved up until her whole body shook. She grabbed the counter as blood rushed from her head, leaving her dizzy. Squeezing her eyes shut and willing herself to stay upright, she held on. The ringing stopped. She stumbled to a kitchen chair and sat down, lowering her head to her arms. Where was he? Had he found her? What was happening?

Dusty splashed quietly as he played in the tub.

The phone chimed. The bastard had left her a message. God, she didn't want to listen to it. Didn't want to hear his awful voice. But she'd kept this number so that she could find out what the man was doing. She had no choice.

She got up to grab the phone, fearing even to touch it, as if the evil in the man made it a dangerous thing. Tossing the instrument onto the table, she took a few moments to gather her courage. Her hands trembled as she called her voicemail.

His hateful voice rasped, "Me again, bitch. You didn't think I forgot about you, did you? Not a chance. No, I've been busy. Busy, busy, busy. I talked to people. Found a place where you worked. And I'll keep coming. I have so many plans for you. If you think we had fun last time, just you wait. Think about that, bitch. I'm on my way. You'll never see me coming."

She bit her lip hard to still the moan of fear that welled up in her throat. The bastard was right. He had all the advantages. There was no way to see him coming.

Lying in bed that night, she tossed and turned, unable to put Blacke's distorted face out of her mind. Too restless, fearing Dusty might wake up, she tiptoed into the bathroom, where she examined herself in the small, splotched mirror. Faint scars were visible on her chin, under her eye, and above her cheekbone. Most people said they didn't notice them much, but to her, they were obvious. A third-year resident in plastic surgery had been on call when she was taken to the E.R., or her face could have been so much worse.

What did Ramsey see when he looked at her? She sighed and splashed her face, drying it before heading into the kitchen and pouring herself a glass of water from the fridge. On edge, she stepped outside and sat on the steps.

The night had settled against a distant half-moon, and the trees in the pasture stirred in a soft breeze. The inky sky was pricked with stars. They had been her friends on many a night like this, and she needed them now. Leaning back against the door, she stared over her head, making patterns where there were none, taking her mind away from the things she couldn't face.

Breathing in deeply, she eased it out, waited for a count of five, then did the same thing again, and then again. This relaxation technique was her old standby, one that had helped her in the past when her personal demons kept her up at night.

In those days, Blacke had been locked safely in prison. *Oh God, what am I going to do?* Despite her best intentions, silent tears slipped down her cheeks.

Crying never helped anything. Despising herself for the weakness, she jerked to her feet, flung the tears from her face, and squared her shoulders.

Craving movement, she walked down the old, warped steps to the road, feeling the breeze brush her arms, cooling her face as it traveled through the pasture and down toward the barn. Shadows of trees and the pale dappled expanse of range grass filled the landscape around her. Everything seemed so strange at night, yet the dark was peaceful.

This dry place was different from, and yet so like the South Texas land she loved. Mesquites made it seem like home, but the wildflowers and wild grasses created a much more attractive environment. She could come to love this country, too, in time.

What about Ramsey? *Ward,* she corrected herself. She'd better get used to calling him that now. He'd been a surprise tonight, actually trying to be nice. She'd liked the way he'd accepted Dusty's offer of throwing the ball. The guy earned points for going down for the eye-level hug, too. That really made her son's night. It killed her to think of the pain her boy would feel when this job was over. All ranch jobs ended, though. Rare was the hand who stayed on at the same place for years.

She yawned. The stars in their dark home had done their work. And now she had a plan. Sleep shouldn't evade her any longer. Heading back inside, she locked the door. She wasn't looking forward to the dawn.

AS SHE SAT WITH DUSTY in the truck down at the bus stop, she silently went over what she needed to do—what to say and how to say it. She hated people feeling sorry for her, so she never shared her troubles. But Blacke was dangerous. If he was coming, she had to tell Ward.

The bus drove off with her son on board, and she turned around, heading to the barn. When her boss pulled up, she was still mulling over her problem. Dropping the bucket of feed, she walked out to meet him. *God, please don't let him send me packing.*

Her face set in a hard, determined expression; she looked him in the eye. "Need to talk to you for a bit."

Ward blinked and then frowned. "Go ahead." Crossing his arms, he settled back on his heels, ready to listen.

Was she doing the right thing? This might pull the man into Blacke's deadly aim. It was selfish. But she had Dusty's safety to consider. That came before anything else.

With her hands in her back pockets, she said, "I got a call last night. There's big trouble on my trail. I don't know when—or if—it'll get here, but I figured I should tell you. If you want us gone, we'll leave here tonight. It's only fair."

Ward narrowed his eyes, as if trying to assimilate the information. "What kind of trouble?"

"I'd say the worst kind. My testimony put a man in prison for cattle rustling, among other things, nine years ago. They let him out early. He threatened to kill me, and he left me a voice mail saying that he had found a ranch I worked at after he went to jail. I know he'll follow through on his threat."

She swallowed and looked down, kicking a rock with her boot. She looked back up. "He's mean as a snake. I figure he'll find me now that he's come looking."

Ward nodded and stayed quiet, looking past her, thinking. In a while, he turned back to her, his lips pulled tight. "You stay. We'll make do. We may change up how things work around here a little, is all."

Nodding once, she said, "All right. Thanks. I mean that." As she picked up the bucket and poured it into the feed trough for the cows, the knot of anxiety in her belly relaxed. She owed her boss now, and owed him big.

He came back down to the barn thirty minutes later with a bundle in the crook of his arm. "Do you have a gun?"

"No, just my skinning knife. I don't like guns." She'd had no use for them since a cowhand on her dad's ranch had killed himself messing around with one when she was a teenager.

"Do you know how to use one, though?"

"Yeah, I learned how to shoot growing up. I don't keep a gun because of Dusty."

He held up a .38 revolver in a tie-down holster. He kept a couple of revolvers around for the infrequent times he needed something besides a rifle. A revolver could be left loaded for long periods of time, unlike a weapon with a magazine where the spring could go bad, causing the gun to jam. Handing her the revolver, he said, "I think you should wear this. Teach the boy how it works and answer all his questions. Then tell him he's not to touch it without your permission. He's a smart kid. He'll be all right."

Hesitating for a few seconds, she took a deep breath and reached for the revolver. She pulled it out of the holster and flipped it open. The chambers were full. Snapping it shut, she chewed her lip. What did they say about desperate times?

Ward said, "I'm licensed to carry. I have a friend who teaches classes. I already made the call. He'll give you a private class tomorrow. We'll get you licensed too. And Jayme? Shoot to kill."

Through clenched teeth, she answered, "I will."

"Okay. It'll probably take the bastard a bit to figure out where you are, but we'll start today acting like he's close. Dusty doesn't play outside unattended, agreed?"

"Hell, yeah. I've already been doing that."

"The times you're around the homeplace, I'll try to be here as well. It won't be easy for him to spy on you leaving the drive because he has no place to hide for a long way either side. Still, be careful when you head out to work someplace else. Be aware of traffic behind you, maybe following you. Okay? Call me if you get suspicious of anything. Also, we need to go talk to the sheriff. Today."

Her eyes narrowed. She didn't like that idea. But this second phone call was a game changer. Blacke had actually found her trail. He was coming.

At her expression, Ward held up his hand. "We don't have a choice. If we have to take matters into our own hands, we want the law to know beforehand that this guy was out to get you and why."

He was right. She knew all too well the kind of man Blacke was. Something would happen, and it wouldn't be good. "Let's go."

FOR THE FIRST TIME, Jayme relaxed with Ward as they drove into town. Somehow, in the past half hour, he'd become her guardian angel. She was almost afraid to say it, but maybe he was becoming her friend. A different kind of warmth spread through her at that thought.

Ward parked at the historic Haskell County Courthouse. When they entered the building, they wound their way through deserted hallways back to the sheriff's office, where Ward asked to speak with Sheriff Bryant. The desk sergeant told them to take a seat in the old, upright wooden chairs along the wall.

Jayme paced, her hands in her back pockets and her pulse racing. Would the sheriff be able to help, or would he be useless, waiting until Blacke actually hurt her again before doing anything to protect her? She'd read stories about that with stalkers. Maybe this whole thing would be a bust.

A door finally opened and a tall, spare man with shrewd blue eyes and wearing a gray Stetson walked through it. "How can I help you today, Ward?"

Her boss shook hands and motioned to Jayme to step a little closer. "Connor, this is Jayme Bonner, my ranch hand. We need to talk to you about a situation that's come up."

The sheriff's no-nonsense appearance reassured her. She offered her hand. "Pleased to meet you, Sheriff."

He shook her hand. "Let's go on back where we can sit down, and we'll see what's what."

They followed him to the door of a small, neat office overwhelmed by an old, beat-up wooden desk.

The sheriff waved them in, and they squeezed into the two guest chairs wedged in front of the desk.

Ward, a solid wall of security at her side, spoke up. "We decided we ought to bring you in on this because we'll probably need some help when the time comes. Jayme, why don't you tell the sheriff what you told me?"

She gave the basic facts, finishing with, "He's a mean one. I can personally vouch for that, Sheriff. He's said he'd kill me, and I believe for sure he'll try." The sheriff listened intently; he seemed to be taking this seriously. Maybe he could help her after all.

She handed him the parole letter, and he took it and made a copy. When he came back, he said, "I'll pull what I can on him. Then I'll call his parole officer and tell him that Blacke has been making threatening phone calls and is stalking you."

Frowning, she said, "If you do that, and he says anything to Blacke, he'll know where I am."

The sheriff held up his hand. "I'll make sure the officer knows not to tell him anything about our location. Don't worry, we've done this before."

For the first time, Jayme was putting her life and the life of her son into someone else's hands, and it didn't feel good. A shiver ran up her spine, and she clasped her hands together to keep them from shaking.

Ward told the sheriff the precautions they'd be taking from then on, including the fact that they would both be legally armed.

The sheriff sighed loudly. "I understand. After I receive the guy's sheet, we'll have a picture of him. My deputies will be on the lookout. I'll let you know if we find him."

As the sheriff rose to his feet, Ward nodded and stood. "Thanks, Connor. We appreciate it."

They shook hands all around, and she and Ward walked out the door, winding their way through the hallway and out to the parking lot.

She glanced at Ward as they headed back to the ranch. "Thanks." It was sinking in. Blacke was coming. He could kill her—kill Dusty. Ward was putting himself in the line of fire for her. What was making him do it? They were practically strangers. Yet he was willing to die to keep her and Dusty safe. Strong emotion washed through her. She'd never felt so cared for. Certainly not with her father. She owed this strange, aloof man. How would she ever repay him?

She squeezed her hands together, chewing her lower lip. Only one thing bothered her. Now her location could be leaked. She was no longer safe at Ward's ranch.

Chapter Seven

The phone rang as Ward was eating his lunch at the kitchen table. Raising his brows, he answered it. "Hi, Annie, what's going on?"

"Casey told me you have a woman and her son living over there now, helping out."

Lord, was she going to give him advice, too? He took a swallow from his bottle of water, and said, "Yeah, I do. Her name is Jayme, and her boy's eight. His name's Dusty."

"They're staying at the old cabin you have over there, right? No TV or anything?"

"Yep, only place to stay here on the ranch."

"Well, I was thinking. We have a little TV/DVD combo that Kylie used to have in her room. She watches her laptop now. And we've got lots of kids' movies my two don't use anymore. I was wondering if the boy would like to have it all. Must be mighty lonely there for him."

When she took a breath, he knew she had more to say. And, knowing Annie, it would be deep into his business.

"Why don't you bring those two over here?"

Yep, he was right.

She barged right on. "You all are invited for dinner Saturday. That boy and David aren't so different in age. Casey said he's a good kid."

"Yeah, he is." He hesitated. "I don't know, Annie."

"Come on. You'd better show up. I'll drop the TV and stuff over later on this afternoon. I'm going to town, so I'll be out and about."

"Okay. Just give me a call when you're on your way over. Thanks for thinking of him."

When he hung up, he scooted his chair back from the table. Annie meant well. Like Casey, she worried about him. Wanted him to be happy. He couldn't be mad at her. But this invitation? That put things on a whole new level.

It was one thing to have Jayme and Dusty living here on the ranch. Inviting them into his personal life was a different matter altogether. The knot in his stomach twisted his gut. No, this dinner was not a good idea.

His gaze traveled around the kitchen with its white, glassed-in cabinets and old Mexican-tiled countertops. Not much had changed from when his mother had reigned here. More than any place in the house, this room was home to him.

Elizabeth and Caleb had never lived here. His parents had both still been alive at the time of the accident, and he and his wife had rented a small house in town while he put away money to build their own home on the ranch.

A couple of years after he'd lost his family, his father had died of a heart attack. Nobody had seen it coming, and his mom had been devastated. While still at the funeral, she'd told him she wanted to switch homes with him. The big, old house he grew up in held too many memories for her.

So he'd moved out to the ranch, and his mother had moved into town, to the rental house where he and Elizabeth had lived when Caleb was born. Ward smoothed his hand across the worn wooden tabletop. The move had been right for him too. He was less haunted here.

Rubbing the day's stubble on his jaw, he considered the trouble following Jayme. That had been a shock. He found it hard to imagine what her life had been like these past nine years. No way would he let that bastard get to her while she lived on his place. No damn way. As much as he'd initially wished that he'd never hired her, he'd come to care for that boy of hers, despite himself. And Jayme had earned his respect. When it came down to it, he didn't want her to leave either. They just had to be careful, that was all. The convict was dealing with someone his own size now, not a vulnerable woman with a boy to protect.

The old kitchen chair creaked as he pushed up and stood tall, arching his back and stretching his spine. The stock in his pasture out past Rule should be checked. Tomorrow he'd head over toward Rochester and see how those cattle were faring, too.

Every fence he owned was in sorry shape and, for some reason, he'd let it slide. There were other things that needed attention as well.

He'd been in a rut—and not a happy one. The time had come to put things right around here. Like coming out of a bad dream, he was ready to get the ranch in shape again. Whatever was responsible for the change in his attitude, he was glad of it. His daddy had taken care of this place, as had his daddy before him, and, dammit, he wouldn't let this ranch fall apart on his watch.

He stepped out into the noonday heat and headed for his truck. He wanted to be back at the homeplace in time for

Dusty's bus. As part of their new routine, it needed to become a habit before Blacke had time to come up this way.

JAYME PARKED AT THE end of the dusty ranch lane and sat waiting for the bus. The sun's baking heat poured in through her open window, and sweat trickled between her breasts. As soon as he got in the truck, Dusty began babbling about his day. She loved that time with him. He always dove into the cooler that held his snack and talked with his mouth full the whole way back. This was the only time she didn't admonish him.

As they headed back toward the barn, Ward's truck appeared in the rearview mirror, turning down the lane from the main road. When they got out at the barn, she motioned for Dusty to follow her. "I'm not setting you up for your homework. I've got to mend fence around here today, and you can come along with me."

Dusty peered at her. "Something wrong, Mom?"

He was too sensitive to her moods not to notice. She figured the boy would worry if she told him and worry more if she didn't.

"I sent a man to prison nine years ago, and he's out now. I hoped he'd forget about me, but I guess he hasn't." She smiled to reassure her son. "He'll come here eventually. I want us to stick close together from here on out."

She bit her lower lip, deciding on how to proceed. "There's something else." Pulling back the denim overshirt she wore as protection from the sun, she exposed the gun belt slung casually across her right hip and the holster which held the dark-handled .38 revolver tied on her thigh. "I'll be wearing this from now on, and it'll take some getting used to. I'll show it to you tonight. You're never to come near the thing or touch it unless I'm with you. Hear me?"

Dusty walked over to her and eyed the gun in its holster. "Wow, Mom. It's just like in the movies. Do you know how to shoot it?"

"Yeah, your grandpa taught me."

Staring hard at him, she said, "You hear me, boy, about not touching this thing?" He minded her well, but still, it'd be a worry. She didn't like guns around the house, and that wouldn't change.

"Yeah, I won't."

"Okay, so finish your snack and then we'll work on that fence. I brought a hat along for you. The sun's hot out there."

Dusty helped her stretch fence, fetched things for her, and played close by while she worked, all without a word of complaint.

The solid weight of the gun at her hip was reassuring. It lessened her anxiety, something she hadn't expected it to do. She had a fighting chance against that bastard Blacke now if he found her. She hadn't realized how defenseless and exposed she'd been feeling until she buckled on the holster and cinched it snug on her thigh.

After they'd been at it for a while, she nudged her son. "So, you scared or anything?"

Dusty tugged on a piece of barbed wire as she tightened it up. When he could let go, he said. "I guess so. What does this man look like, Momma?"

"He's got yellow hair and brown eyes, kind of like you. Probably has some muscles now that he's been in prison. Those guys usually work out."

"I'll watch for him."

She pulled off her hat and wiped the sweat gathered at the band. "Good. You yell real loud if you ever see him, okay?" *Oh God, please don't let Blacke get close to my boy.*

He nodded vigorously.

Poor baby, she hated to scare him like this. And one thing really worried her: now that he knew, would her son have nightmares like his momma?

WHILE JAYME AND DUSTY were finishing dinner that night, a vehicle pulled up outside. They stared wide-eyed at each other before she got up and peeked out the window. "We're okay. It's Mr. Ramsey." Her tummy did a little flutter of anticipation as Ward walked around to the passenger side of his truck. When he came back into view, he was holding a small television set and two plastic grocery bags.

She opened the door and backed away, feeling his powerful, masculine presence acutely as he stepped inside.

His face softened as he laid eyes on her son.

What would it be like to brush her lips against his chiseled mouth? She sighed. He'd been affecting her like this more and more, and it was no good. The man was her boss, for cripes' sake. The last thing she needed to do was fall for him.

Dusty stood close, an expectant look on his face. "Hi, Mr. Ramsey. Whatcha got there?"

"A friend of mine sent this over for you. Used to belong to her daughter. She has a boy near your age, too. They thought you might like to see some TV now and then."

Dusty trailed his fingers down the side of it and then looked up, a huge grin on his face. "Mom, a TV. Do we get TV out here?"

She smiled and ran her fingers through his curls. No, they sure didn't, but it looked like Ward had something else in mind. Her boy was going to be so happy.

Ward set the TV down on the floor. "Well, not really, but that's why they also sent these." Handing the boy one of the bags, he said, "This is full of movies. I'll show you how to use it."

Ward looked at her, sending tiny shivers skittering up her torso. The man showing kindness to her son was a real turn-on for her.

"Where do you want to set this up?" Ward asked.

Ignoring her body's reaction to him, she scanned around the nearly bare room and then pulled the small coffee table closer to the wall and the outlet there. "How about here?" She kept her distance. The man's rocking-hot body was doing all sorts of crazy things to her today.

"That should work for now. I'll bring an extension cord and then you can move it nearer the couch. It has a pretty small screen." He called Dusty over, showing him how to turn the TV on and put in a DVD. Then he walked him through using the remote control.

Her boy was awestruck.

She smiled at the two of them, heads together, focused on the task. They were so damned cute.

Ward ruffled Dusty's hair.

She wanted to kiss the man. Did he have any idea how much her boy needed touches like that? She found herself liking Ward, given the changes in him over the past couple of weeks. It made it easier to accept the way her heart leapt in her chest every time she laid eyes on him. His previous hard-assed attitude had worn her down more each day she'd had to put up with it.

This TV would make a world of difference, and she was thankful to Ward's friend and to Ward. It was something she couldn't have given Dusty on her own.

He chose *Milo and Otis*, a movie about a runaway puppy and kitten.

She laid the movie case down and walked over to the big picture window in the room, staring out at the distant, flat horizon. This job was a good one. She liked that Ward allowed her time to do her work. Being rushed and forced to do something half-assed had never suited her. Here, her boss expected things to be done well. And now that he was less harsh, she didn't mind working for him.

The man was kind to her son. That meant the world to her. She had a nice little house to live in, could pick up Dusty from the bus, and had a boss she could respect. All that went a long way toward making this job one she wanted to stay with.

When she turned around, Dusty's eyes were glued to the beginning of the movie, but Ward's intense gaze was on her. Her heart thumped at the surprising warmth in it. Nodding to him, she said, "Thanks for this. I don't know how to repay you."

"No need. My friend Annie sent these over. She wants you and Dusty to come to dinner Saturday too."

"Been a while since we went anywhere for dinner. Hope my son remembers his manners."

The corners of Ward's eyes crinkled. "Your boy will be fine. How about his momma?"

Grinning, she said, "I guess I deserved that. I promise not to call you a you-know-what anymore." The man looked positively delectable with that mischievous look on his face. She was finding it harder and harder to see him as her tough-guy boss and easier to see him as a sexy man, especially when he looked at her that way. She couldn't remember when she'd last felt attracted like this.

After Blacke, she'd felt nothing but horror for years. When that faded, she'd felt—what? More interest in her son and in being a good mom and putting food on the table. And distrust when a man moved into her personal space. She'd known it wasn't right, but the distrust was there anyway. Somehow, maybe through his kindness to her son, Ward had gotten past that.

Ward grinned and patted Dusty's shoulder. "I'll see you later. You have fun."

Dusty tore his eyes from the TV long enough to hug Ward's waist.

He bent and hugged him back before heading out the front door.

Jayme enjoyed the view as he walked out to his truck and climbed in. The man wasn't such a tough guy after all. Things were better between them now, but she couldn't let her growing attraction to him change anything. He was still her boss.

WARD PULLED UP TO THE ranch house and put the truck in park. What in the hell had just happened? It was like his mouth had a mind of its own. Didn't he decide the dinner invitation was a bad idea? He clearly remembered telling himself he wouldn't invite Jayme and Dusty into his personal life, and now he'd gone and done it anyway. Clenching his teeth, he switched off the engine. It was a sad day when a man had no self-control. He got out of the truck and slammed the door, striding into the house.

The following Saturday afternoon, he arrived at Jayme's, as prepared as he would ever be to take them to the barbeque at Casey's. As he got out of his truck, he prayed that the evening wouldn't be as awkward as he feared.

Dusty threw open the door, grabbed him around the waist, and hugged him tight.

He knelt and hugged the boy back. "You ready, young man?" At least he had the boy. Dusty always talked. That would make the ride easier.

"Been ready. Mom's the one who took forever."

Jayme appeared in the doorway.

Ward's eyes widened, and his tongue stuck to the roof of his mouth. She'd dressed nicely, but what took his breath away were the dark masses of curls falling around her shoulders, her beautiful green eyes enhanced by shadow, and the curve of her moist, plum-colored lips. And where had those cheekbones been? Holy shit, she was breathtaking.

Heart galloping for the finish line as his body came to attention, he jerked his gaze away, surged to his feet, and grabbed Dusty's hand. "Let's go, sport. Don't want dinner to get cold."

Chapter Eight

Did Jayme have any idea how rocking hot she was? Ward kept up a conversation with Dusty on the drive to Casey's, talking about anything and everything he could think of to keep his mind off the sexy bombshell on the other side of the truck. What the hell would he do all night? How could he stop himself from staring at her like a hound dog in heat? Dammit, Annie!

Thirty minutes later, they pulled into the gravel driveway.

Annie came out the front door to greet them. "Hey, you all, come on inside. We're eating out back."

He helped the boy down as she walked up. "Annie, this is Dusty, the young man I told you about."

"I'm so glad to finally meet you."

Dusty grinned and put out his hand. "Thank you, Miss Annie. I love the TV and movies. I never had a TV of my own."

Ward was way too aware of Jayme walking around the truck and stopping beside him. She was even wearing perfume. Was she trying to drive him nuts?

Annie shook Dusty's hand and turned to her other guest. "You must be Jayme. I'm so happy you could come. I'll bet you've been dying to talk to someone besides this old coot."

Jayme grinned. "You got that right."

They headed into the house. The scent of cooking beans and homemade bread wafted around him. He was last in line, the view of Jayme's fine rear-end a distraction as they wound their way through the living room and kitchen.

As they came out on the porch, Casey said. "Welcome. Food should be done in about thirty minutes." He put his barbeque fork down and walked over to meet the newcomers.

Ward gestured to Jayme. "This is my new hand, Jayme Bonner. Jayme, this is Casey, a no-account old reprobate I've known since grade school." He eyed his friend, wondering what he was going to say. He always found a way to gig Ward, if given half a chance.

She laughed. "I'd like to hear what you call him. I'm sure it's much better."

Casey went back to the grill and raised the lid. The tantalizing smell of steaks and the sound of sizzling fat rose with it. He turned to her and said, "Excuse me in advance. I'm sure you're polite company. My favorite name for him is Asshole."

Jayme pursed her lips. "Appropriate, yes...very appropriate."

Ward grinned.

Dusty, who'd lagged behind everyone else to pet an old Blue Heeler, walked over.

Ward introduced the boy. "This big guy is Dusty. He's turned into quite a fisherman. And he's got a pretty good arm on him, too. Speaking of which, I'll be right back." Ward had anticipated this for several days and couldn't wait to see the look on Dusty's face when he returned.

The boy scrunched his brows together as Ward disappeared into the house.

In a few minutes, he reappeared with three baseball mitts in his hands. He handed one to Dusty, one to Jayme, and kept one for himself. "Now, we're all set to throw whenever you have a hankering, Dusty. How about you and I toss to each other?" Ward grabbed the new baseball stuffed inside his shirt and threw it to the boy. The look on Dusty's face was priceless.

Dusty carefully put his new glove and ball on the lawn and wrapped his arms around Ward, squeezing him tight.

Ward squatted down and hugged him back hard, cupping his head in his hand and ruffling his hair. "You're a good boy, son, and I expect now you'll get lots better at throwing that ball." Ward smiled. This had been everything he'd hoped it would be.

Dusty drew back and looked him in the eye. "Yes, sir! I will!"

Jayme stood next to Casey, watching Ward zinging the ball back and forth with Dusty.

When she met his gaze, it made him as antsy as a calf weaning from his momma. Her breasts, her rounded butt—everything about her said *hold me; kiss me*. He turned away. *How will I ever work beside her again? Tonight changes everything.*

When she sat on the other side of the patio, he settled down. Until dinner was served, that is.

They were using the picnic table in the shade of the oak tree. Annie put Jayme right next to him. The bench was a tight squeeze, and several times during dinner his thigh brushed hers. Desire surged through him, stirring what shouldn't be stirred. He was reacting like a high-school boy on his first hot date.

Jayme leaned forward, and her T-shirt hugged her beautifully formed breasts.

He nearly choked and tore his eyes from her chest. The third time he bumped her, he stifled a groan and got up. Anything to put some space between them.

JAYME GLANCED AT WARD. Without saying a word, he strode into the house. That wasn't unusual for—what had Annie called him? The old coot.

She actually enjoyed sitting close to him. It was kind of like losing her wall of security when he stood and walked away. When he came back a few minutes later, he slid into the seat beside her without looking in her direction. Man, this guy was like hot and cold water. Would she ever get used to his mood swings?

Ward hadn't said two words to her since her introduction. But she was enjoying getting to know Casey and Annie. She hadn't had real friends in a long time. This evening, it was easy to forget Blacke and the terror he instilled in her.

After dinner, they all cleaned up the remnants of the meal and sat around talking. Dusty and David were inside watching one of David's new movies. Relaxed in her chair, cool in the evening breeze as she sipped her beer, she couldn't remember ever feeling this happy, this content.

Annie raised her beer and pointed to Jayme. "We need to do a girls' day one weekend and go to Wichita Falls. I'll bet you could talk Ward into staying with your boy."

Ward's eyes widened and blinked, and then he nodded. "Sure, Dusty and me can hang out while you ladies entertain yourselves."

No longer worried about her son being alone with her boss, she said, "I'm in, Annie. I don't think I've ever had a girls' day."

"Well, it's about time then, hon."

The evening wound down. She rounded up Dusty and they loaded into the truck with fond goodbyes. The boy was drowsy on the way home, leaning into her shoulder, but keeping up a sleepy monologue about his new friend. Was this how normal people lived? Never once had she and her father done something like this when she was growing up. Occasionally, at one of the ranches she'd worked at, the foreman's wife had invited her and Dusty to dinner. But it wasn't like having an evening with friends, like tonight. This had been an entirely unique experience. And absolutely wonderful.

Her boy had had one of the best evenings of his life, too. She glanced over at Ward. He sat relaxed, wrist resting on the steering wheel. This man had made the evening possible. The tab she owed her guardian angel just kept getting longer. She was beginning to like Ward—a lot.

Ward glanced Dusty's way several times as the boy talked. He was smiling, but he never quite looked at her.

As they pulled up at the little cabin, she realized Dusty had fallen sound asleep. Ward motioned for her to get out, and he picked up the boy, meeting her at the front door. The picture he made, holding her son in his arms, sent warm fuzzies straight to her heart. Leading Ward through to the bedroom, she managed to pull the covers down in the dim light from the door.

Ward laid him in the bed and removed his boots. She slipped Dusty's jeans off, tucking the blanket up under his chin. Before backing away, she placed a kiss on his forehead. To her astonishment, Ward bent, added his own gentle kiss on her son's cheek, and walked quietly out.

With a lump in her throat, she followed Ward out through the front door and down the steps. A strong breeze swept her hair back from her face, and crickets sounded loud in the night. As he headed toward his truck, she called him back. She hadn't turned the porch light on, and he stood near her in the darkness, lit only by the moon.

Her heart rate quickening, she struggled to find the right words. "Ward, thanks for inviting us tonight."

He opened his mouth.

She held up her hand. There was so much she wanted to say, and she wanted to get it right. "I know Annie invited us, but you didn't have to agree. This evening was wonderful for Dusty. It showed him what normal families do." Ward's eyes, dark pools in the moonlight, told her nothing of his feelings.

Hesitating, she reached out and took his hand, covering it with her own. "I can't thank you enough for that." She squeezed and let it go, feeling a great warmth for him.

Ward was quiet for a couple of seconds before he spoke. "You're welcome, Jayme. I'm sorry I'm such an asshole. I've been an asshole for a long time. I think now that I know you and Dusty, I'll be less of one. I hope, anyway. You both deserve better."

She hadn't expected those words and she wasn't sure what to say, except, "Thank you, Ward. Goodnight." Stepping back, she tripped on the step behind her, tumbling backward.

"Jayme!" Ward snatched her to him, saving her from a nasty fall.

Dammit to hell! A hot flush swept up her neck and face. Then a whole new world of sensation assailed her. The scent of warm leather and oak, his aftershave, filled her nostrils. The sound of a strong heart beat steadily against her ear. Enveloped in a cocoon of comfort and security, she stood completely still in Ward's protective embrace.

Drawing back, she opened her mouth to thank Ward for saving her—and found him staring intently at her in the dim light.

His arms still encircled her. His wonderful scent engulfed her. She thought of Dusty, of how sweet Ward was to her boy, and suddenly she knew what she wanted to do. Standing on her tiptoes, she placed a light kiss on his warm, firm lips and eased back.

As she settled to her heels again, Ward gently cupped her face in his calloused hand. A ghost of a smile touched his mouth as he ran his thumb across her lip. "Goodnight, Jayme. I enjoyed tonight." He turned slowly on his heel and headed for his truck.

Where had this gentle, sexy man been? And, God, how long had it been since she felt a man's arms around her? Her skin burned where his hand had touched her. Hand at her throat, she stared after him as he drove away.

THE NEXT MORNING AT eight o'clock, Ward still sat at the kitchen table, drinking a third cup of coffee. What was he going to do? He was Jayme's boss, and he was full-on attracted to her.

Lord, he'd been aroused when he got home last night. He thought of all sorts of things he wanted to do and say to Jayme. If only she didn't work for him. If only he weren't responsible for her and Dusty.

She felt so perfect in his arms. He hadn't expected that. Sure, she was beautiful, but the woman was more than that. And he needed—wanted—to find out what made her tick. What drove a woman like her into the rough life of a ranch hand? Why was she alone? How had she managed on her own with a small child? He wanted to know all of this and more.

He headed outside, still at a loss, and drove down to the barn. He hoped Jayme had her head on straight about their relationship. He sure didn't.

JAYME TURNED AS WARD walked in, the sun at his back outlining his tall, lean, muscular form. Something thrilled inside her. Having already fed the animals, she was leaning on the pipe railing and looking into a stall where one of their oldest cows had given birth overnight. She examined his expression, looking for clues.

Ward came over and crossed his arms on top of the rail. "Good morning. I see you've fed already."

She was intensely aware of his strong body next to hers. His clean scent at this close proximity all but overwhelmed her supercharged senses. "I imagine. You're late, boss."

"Yeah, I uh, Jayme... Well, hell, I've never had a woman work here before, you know?" He frowned, his brows drawn together in concern. "I don't want to take advantage... What I mean is—I'm your boss. Last night..." He looked down and shoved his hands in his pockets.

Lifting her head so he could see her eyes, she said, "Hey, I took advantage of you, if you'll remember." The corner of her mouth quirked up. "I kissed you." She reached out and patted his arm. "Thank you for worrying." Aw, was he really a sweetheart underneath that badass exterior?

He laughed. "Right."

"So, what are my marching orders today, boss?" They got that settled, and she took a deep breath as she walked toward her horse, Rowdy's, pen. Ward had taken the first step, and they'd talked about last night. It remained to be seen how it affected her job, though. Would he still treat her as a professional, or would he start treating her like a girl? Shit, she *hated* being treated like a girl. She threw her head back and groaned. She'd broken her cardinal rule—*never get involved with a man on your ranch.*

That afternoon, she sat at the end of the ranch-house drive, a brisk, hot wind kicking up a dust devil in the pasture beside her. Dusty's school bus was a few minutes late, but her mind was on something else entirely—the way she was beginning to feel about her boss. She rubbed her hands up and down her arms, biting her lower lip.

As Ward had held her wrapped in his tight embrace, her body had hummed with excitement, flushing warm as she melted into his hard muscles. Safety had curled around her, and she hadn't wanted the moment to end.

Now, much as she tried, she couldn't think of Ward the way she used to. When she saw him, she wasn't looking at her supervisor anymore. Instead, she faced the man her body remembered with desire, the man who smelled of leather and oak, the man who now taunted her with things she shouldn't want from a boss. Everything had changed.

If these thoughts, these feelings, were happening to her, couldn't those same things be bothering him? She groaned long and low. What an awful thought. How could they work together? She had to get a handle on her attraction to him. This mess couldn't put her job in jeopardy. She must keep sanctuary for herself and Dusty as her one and only goal.

Chapter Nine

Annie had finally taken Jayme for their girls' day out, and the woman was a hoot. Jayme had laughed so much during their time together that her sides hurt. She'd never met anyone so open, so happy, so trusting, as her friend. Jayme couldn't help wondering what kind of family Annie had grown up in. It had to have been full of love and acceptance.

Night had fallen, and her phone showed it was nearly eight-thirty—much later than she'd planned on arriving home. She'd just called Ward and told him she'd be there shortly.

Her boss was a natural at caring for her son. He had a key to her house and, after feeding Dusty, he'd taken him home and sent him in for his bath. Apparently, her boy was now reading to Ward on the couch, getting in a few extra minutes with his idol before bedtime.

Annie turned her attention from the road for a second. "Ward's changed since you all moved in. He's happier."

Jayme nodded. "He's turned into a good boss, and he's great with Dusty."

Annie glanced at her again. "But what? I hear a 'but' there somewhere."

"I just worry about things, is all." *Like how will my son handle losing him when my job here ends? As all ranch jobs do, this one will finish someday, and how can I protect Dusty?*

"Well, I realize Ward is a hard man to get to know, but I think you'll find he's worth it. He'll be good for you. And good for Dusty too."

Jayme lifted the corner of her mouth and nodded, then turned and leaned her forehead against the window. Dusty had gotten closer to Ward than any man before him. The pain of losing him would be agonizing for her boy.

DUSTY HAD FALLEN ASLEEP with his head on Ward's shoulder. One minute he was listening to Ward's fishing story, and the next thing he was sleeping. Ward sat very still, rubbing his hand up and down the boy's back, cherishing the way Dusty's small body melted into his. The sweet, clean scent of his hair filled Ward's nose and brought back memories of another small boy who had nestled in his arms. Tonight, that memory wasn't so hard to bear. A quiet groan passed his lips. How could it be wrong to hold this child?

Tires made a crackling sound on the gravel outside as Annie's SUV drove in. Anticipation sent Ward's heart racing as he realized Jayme was home.

A few minutes later, she walked through the door and, seeing Dusty's sleeping form, tiptoed over.

He nodded toward the bedroom and gathered the boy in his arms. His limp, fragile form tugged at Ward's heart, and he gripped him tighter.

Jayme turned down the covers and he tucked Dusty in, then kissed him goodnight.

After giving her son her own kiss, she quietly shut the door and headed into the living room.

He turned to Jayme, glad she was home, having anticipated it all day. "How was—"

"Would you—"

They grinned at each other.

Jayme gestured to the kitchen. "How about a beer, Mr. Babysitter?"

"Sure. I'd like that." Lord, she looked good as she walked away from him, her perfectly curved hips swinging with her stride.

She got them both a beer and motioned to Ward to sit on the couch with her. The silent house created a cocoon of intimacy around them. "So, tell me how my son tortured you today, boss."

He laughed. Jayme appeared so happy and relaxed. And sexy-hot, with her hair curling over her shoulders and remnants of lipstick highlighting her full lips. He had to stop and think to remember her question. "No torture at all. We went around to a couple of the pastures and then stopped for an ice cream."

"You're spoiling him."

The smile that lit Jayme's face did something odd to Ward's chest. It felt as though his heart skipped a beat. "No way. The kid worked hard for it. Of course, we couldn't go to town without stopping for a donut."

"What? Ice cream *and* a donut? I'm surprised you got him to sleep tonight."

Her breasts rose and fell slightly with each breath, and desire surged through him. She was so beautiful she made him hurt, and he was having a terrible time following the conversation. "He burned all that energy, believe me. By talking, if nothing else. Where does he get all those questions?"

Jayme grinned. "Tell me about it. Thank goodness for Google."

He sipped his beer, and silence lay easily between them. He wanted more than this. More than sharing a beer and going home to his empty house. What would it be like if the three of them were at home—a real family? His eyes narrowed as a sharp pang of guilt hit him, yet a tiny part of him yearned for that scenario.

He reached out his hand, encouraging Jayme to move over beside him.

Her eyes bored into him as she furrowed her brows.

With no idea what she was thinking, he'd almost decided he'd overstepped his bounds when her face relaxed and she scooted over next to him.

He slipped his fingers through hers, and his chest tightened as her shoulder touched his. This was what he wanted.

Squeezing her hand, he said. "So, tell me a little about Jayme Bonner. What's your family like? Do you have any brothers and sisters? Parents wondering about their tough daughter out wandering the wilds of Texas?"

Her mouth set in a firm line. "My dad raised me. He's a foreman on a large ranch in south Texas, where I was raised. My mom died when I was four. I don't remember much about her, but she sang to me and kissed me—I know she loved me."

She took a deep breath and let it out. "I figured maybe my father loved me, but he never showed it if he did. I might have reminded him too much of my mom. Instead of affection, he taught me ranching. Everything I know. I grew up starved for a man's love, just like my boy." She looked off through the window and into the night.

He squeezed her hand. So that was what made her so tough. "But Dusty has you. Even if his dad's not around, you love him."

Smiling, she said, "I love him enough for two, that's for sure. I try to make up for his losses, best I can."

"So where is Dusty's daddy? Does he help you at all?"

She frowned. "He's not in the picture, and I prefer it that way."

A few seconds later, she squeezed his hand. "I like you, Ward Ramsey. Thanks so much for watching my boy today."

Her words, her touch, her smell, sent shivers skittering through him. He wanted to pull her into his arms and brand those lovely lips as his own. He sucked in a sharp breath, needing his wildly drumming pulse to slow, needing to get his head straight.

After a hard check to his emotions, he smiled. "Thank you. That means a lot to me, especially after the way I've treated you."

She turned to him. "So, what makes tough-guy Ward Ramsey tick? Do you have brothers and sisters? What about your parents?"

Her eyes, usually so intent and focused, were warm and interested. A smile played across her lips. Why had he waited so long to talk to her? Sitting here, having this conversation, felt right. He looked down at her hand, his fingers laced through hers, and something he hadn't felt in a long time swept through him. What was it? He drew his brows together and answered.

"I'm an only child. My mom couldn't have any more kids after what my birth did to her. My father passed away, but my mother lives in Howelton. I go visit her pretty regular, but she doesn't much like coming out to the ranch. She says there are too many memories here."

Jayme nodded. "An only child. We have that in common. I always wanted brothers and sisters. I never had anyone to play with growing up. I feel bad that Dusty's had a lot of that, too." Her eyes narrowed. "Just so you know, I never planned on having him. I never would have dragged a kid around with me like this on purpose. But I've loved him from the minute I knew he was coming, and I'm glad he's mine."

"You're a good mom. Your boy's proof of that."

She smiled, then covered a yawn. "I'm so sorry!" She put her beer on the table.

He stood, reluctant to go, but knowing he should. "I enjoyed the conversation, but it sounds like you need some shut-eye."

She smiled and got to her feet. "I'm sorry. I didn't realize how tiring a girls' day could be. That Annie's a go-getter."

He took her hands, gazing into her eyes as he pulled her gently toward him. Easing her into a warm hug, he held her there. Having every inch of her long body melted against him sent fire shooting through his veins. He drew in his breath and kissed the top of her head. Her dark hair smelled deliciously of floral shampoo. He relaxed his arms and ran his hands a few inches up her back, still holding her loosely. His heart pounded, his hands felt unsteady. This woman rocked him hard.

Her green eyes were wide, blazing into him, drawing him close. He tilted his head and brushed his mouth across hers, feeling a jolt of electricity race through him the instant their lips touched. Deepening the kiss, he enjoyed her taste as her hands slid up his back.

She kissed him back with a gentle touch of her lips.

He stifled a groan, knowing this needed to stop. With a last nip of her bottom lip, he stepped back.

Her dazed expression left no doubt that she was as overwhelmed by the experience as he was.

He pulled her in for another long hug, committing every touch of her body to memory before releasing her. Clasping her face in his hands, he dropped a chaste kiss on her forehead. "I'll see you in the morning."

Driving home, he was still unable to find words for what he was feeling. But, hey, she liked him, huh? It might be his imagination, but he felt his heart expanding, warming his chest. Now he just had to keep her and Dusty safe.

AFTER WARD LEFT, JAYME needed time under the stars. She wanted to laugh with joy and run far, far away at the same time. Being with Ward had been incredible—like lightning surging from him directly to her heart, pulsing and throbbing with each beat. Her lips tingled, remembering his intimate kiss.

Yet everything she had inside her was screaming that this was wrong. She didn't have any idea how to handle this new relationship. Too much was at stake. This job, and the refuge it provided, was critical to her survival.

Sighing, she gazed up at her twinkling friends in the night sky, but they didn't have the answers tonight. She clasped her hands and prayed silently. *God, please protect me and my boy from Blacke. And, please God, show me what's best for me. Ward's a special man, but I don't know what to do. Amen.*

DAYS PASSED IN A BLUR for Jayme. Dusty picked up immediately that things were different. He was ecstatic that his mom liked Mr. Ramsey now.

Saturday morning rolled around, and Ward drove over to the cabin to pick them up.

Dusty trotted over as soon as her boss stepped out of the truck. "Hi, Mr. Ramsey."

Ward smiled and ruffled her son's hair. "Why don't you get on inside and put your seat belt on. I need a word with your mom."

She tilted her head up, slipping her hands into her back pockets. The man was certainly looking happy today. And, oh, so very sexy.

He took off his straw Stetson and held it in his hands. "It's nothing serious. I'm asking you two over for dinner at the house tonight. I wanted to be sure you could decline without disappointing Dusty."

"I appreciate that, but we'd be glad to come. Can I bring anything?" She bit back a smile. That grin of Ward's could light up the whole town.

"Naw, I got it covered. Come on over about six."

He had a definite spring in his step when he turned back to the truck.

As she climbed in on her side, Dusty was bouncing up and down.

"Four cartoon channels, Mom! Mr. Ramsey has four cartoon channels at his house, and we're eating dinner there tonight!"

She laughed. Such small things made him happy. "Whatever will you do? I don't know how you'll decide what to watch. Now put that seat belt on."

Her son frowned, considering.

Ward rescued him as he swung the truck around. "Don't worry. It has a menu that tells you what's playing on each channel. You'll be able to choose real easy."

Dusty sighed, then looked at Ward with wide-open eyes. "How can you go to bed at night with so much stuff on all the time? I couldn't."

Ward laughed. "I guess I'm just used to it. If there's something I really want to see, I can record it and watch it later."

"Wow, I never knew that."

For her son, the morning was full of questions about Ward's house and, of course, cartoons.

HOW HER LIFE HAD CHANGED in just a few short months. School would be out soon, and Dusty would be spending even more time on the ranch. Now that Ward had changed in his attitude toward them, she wasn't dreading that anymore. She looked at the man and her son happily chatting away and felt, for the first time, as though things might turn out all right.

As they came back from feeding at one of the pastures, Dusty stared at the old adobe ranch house. "Did they fight any Indians at your house in the old days?"

Ward had an interesting answer. "The main part of the house was originally built in 1867. It came into our family not long after. There have been some changes to it over the years, but, being that old, it stood off some Indians in its time."

He motioned out the truck window. "I'll put a ladder against the wall sometime so you can climb up high. You'll be able to see a couple of bullet holes that my great-great-grandpa never filled in. He left them as a reminder to all his descendants to stay on their toes."

Pointing to the top of the house, he said. "See those tall square things up along that low wall at the roof line? Those are crenellations. They're put there so a man can kneel behind them and shoot from cover."

Dusty's eyes followed the house until it disappeared from sight.

Ward was so patient with her son, and he really seemed interested in him. This easy, relaxed guy was so different from the tense, hard man she'd met when she first came to the ranch. Her thoughts turned to him throughout her day now, just as she thought about Dusty. It was almost as if they were a family. She gusted out a breath. Whoa there, Nelly. Yes, he was a nice man, but he was also her boss. She rolled her eyes and looked out the window.

When they got back to the cabin, she grinned at Ward. "Go home and stuff some cotton in your ears. It'll help."

He grinned. "Cotton balls. Got it—first on my list."

Waving good-bye, she put her arm around Dusty's shoulders as they walked into the house.

Tonight's dinner invitation had butterflies fluttering in her tummy. She'd come to realize that Ward was different. She was drawn to him like no other man she'd known. He called to a need in her. And she'd finally found a man she could trust.

WARD TOOK SEVERAL PACKAGES of T-bones out of the freezer and opened them up, laying them in the sink to thaw. He wanted tonight to be relaxing for Jayme. From what he could tell, her life had been pretty bleak. As he set some iced tea to steep, his cell phone rang out in the living room.

Accepting the call, he sat down in the recliner. "Hey, Cash, what's up?"

"Nothing much. I was wondering if you wanted to come over for a beer."

Ward leaned his chair back. "I can't. I'm having company." *Here it comes.*

"Ward Ramsey is having company over? Let me write that down on my calendar. It's an event."

"Ha, ha, very funny. I've been known to do it from time to time."

"Not in a long time-to-time. Who is it?"

Ward grimaced. *No way is this up for gossip.* "None of your business, nosy."

Cash laughed. "Okay, I wondered how long it'd take you to ask her out. She's cute. That's what they said in town, anyway."

"Dammit, Cash. Shut the hell up. You gossip like an old lady." Seriously, he needed to make sure Cash kept quiet. He hated gossip about his private life. As a long-time bachelor in a small town, he was always newsworthy.

"I'm just saying. When do I get to meet her?"

"How about never, smart-ass?"

Cash laughed again. "Come on."

"She's a nice woman, and her kid's great. I just thought I'd spend some time getting to know her better."

Cash was quiet a second. "I really would like to meet her sometime. I'm happy for you."

"Thanks, buddy." Jayme was the kind of woman he wouldn't mind introducing to his friends, unlike his friends with benefits that he visited in town on rare occasions.

"Listen, you have fun. It's about time you got a life. We'll catch up soon. And I want details."

He cracked up. "You wish. And keep your trap shut. Bye."

Tonight, he and Jayme would have plenty of time to talk. Dusty would be caught up in his cartoons, and they could chat while he cooked the steaks. He wanted to learn about Jayme—to get to know her past, her life. Without that, it all felt hollow.

He smiled. That boy had been something else today. To think a few kid channels could fire him up like that. Ward couldn't feel bad around Dusty. Who could be pissed off at the world when you could see it through that boy's eyes every day?

Getting to know his momma was much harder. But, as thorny as Jayme Bonner was, she'd gotten under his skin. She'd said she liked him the other night, and that meant a lot coming from a woman like her. Her high regard didn't come easily.

He tried not to think of the way she felt when he held her close. He'd never make it through dinner if he let his mind take him back there. But his body remembered and was already responding. Hot blood charged through him. How could something so simple, so innocent as a hug, feel so erotic?

Shoving the recliner upright, he headed back to shower.

JAYME KNEW SHE WAS in trouble when Ward answered his door, freshly showered and smelling wonderful. An excited Skippy bounced on his hind legs, happy to see them. She sighed. A man that sexy, that blatantly masculine, had surely been made to rock her world. Swallowing hard, she ushered Dusty into the house, her heart pelting away in her chest.

Ward led them through the house. As they passed a darkened hallway, he pointed. "The bathroom is down there and on the right." Patting Dusty's shoulder, he urged him ahead of them into the kitchen. "Would you like some iced tea?"

Her boy grinned. "Yes, sir."

Ward poured him a glass. "Jayme, if you don't mind helping yourself, I believe Dusty and I have an appointment with the cartoon channels."

"Yes!" Dusty pumped his fist in the air and followed Ward from the room.

After pouring a glass of tea, Jayme pulled herself together for a minute in the cozy, old-fashioned kitchen. Spending time with Ward was more overwhelming than she anticipated. Her pulse raced as she took a deep breath. All of these sensations—the heart palpitations, the constant awareness of his presence, her body's traitorous reaction—were new to her. She'd always been happy alone, seldom choosing to spend time with men. She sucked in her bottom lip. Tonight, being here in his house, felt right, though. Tugging her shirt down, she followed the sounds to the living room where Ward was giving directions for the TV remote.

He explained how the cartoon channels were arranged sequentially in the guide.

Dusty made his choice and settled back in the recliner, eyes glued to the television.

Ward's hand on the small of her back sent shivers up her spine as they walked into the kitchen.

He said, "I don't expect we'll see much of him before dinner."

"Not by the look of it, no. I think we have a convert." She heaved a sigh. "Poor guy. He never complains that we don't have real TV. Now I realize how much he misses it." She felt such a failure as a mother sometimes. Living in remote locations, depriving him of playmates and television, made her son's life so solitary.

Ward picked up a tray of seasoned steaks and headed for the back door. "Come on, let's put these on the grill."

He caught her gaze as he forked each steak onto the rack. "He's welcome to come watch TV anytime, Jayme. I'd like to have him visit. This house gets mighty lonely."

Before she could answer, he gestured toward her with the fork. "You're both welcome." His grin turned into a slow, dangerous smile. The kind that turned women's brains into mush.

Tiny quivers of desire spread through her body. Surely he knew what that smile did to the female half of the human population? What did it say that he was using it on her?

"Thank you, Ward. Dusty would love to come down and watch his cartoons. And spend time with you. We might do that." She took a deep breath to clear her head. Her body was responding to him. She wanted to move closer, to get into his personal space. Was this really her?

"Why don't you have a seat in the shade over there?" He motioned with the tray to a couple of chairs under several tall oak trees. "I'll put this inside and grab a glass of tea."

A much safer suggestion. She sat down and tore her gaze away from his perfect backside as he headed into the house. Instead, she admired the panoramic view. The land fell away from the yard down to a large pond, and cattle wended their way across the pasture for their evening drink. A light breeze tickled her cheek as insects filled the air with their sounds.

When he came back out, he hung a plastic grocery bag from a hook on the front of the grill.

"What's that?" She kept her traitorous eyes on his hands.

"My potatoes, wrapped in foil. I'll put them on in a little while. I like them toasty, but not burned. I've cooked them a ways in the microwave already."

She was incredibly aware of him. When he sat beside her, he was so close that her arm brushed his as she sipped her tea. His leather-and-oak scent filled her head with memories of their kisses.

With a gallop, her libido thundered out of the gate. Quickly, she stood. Guessing he was watching her ass, she shoved her hands into her back pockets. It wasn't much of a barrier, but it was all she could think of at the moment. Walking toward the back fence, she watched the cattle, listening to them call as they approached the water.

Turning, she gestured at the barbeque pit. "I've never cooked my potatoes like that. I bet they'll be delicious." After a moment, she headed back to her chair.

Ward smiled as she sat down. "I learned to do them like this in rodeo college. We cooked out a lot back then, and one of the other cowboys showed me."

Careful to keep some distance between them, she raised her brows and asked, "What did you learn in rodeo college, besides the obvious?"

"Well, sure, we had lots of fun. I rodeoed, like everybody else, but that wasn't my most important goal. I wanted to understand ranch management: how to make this place pay, to learn the land and how to take care of it. It's what my degree's in—Agricultural Business Management."

Looking out over the pasture again, she said, "I would have loved to go to college for that. But college was never in the cards for me. No money. I always had the goal to be a ranch foreman, though. I know about the land, rotating crops, fertilizers, changing where and what stock to graze. All of that. But those jobs are rare, and even more so for a woman." She felt the pang of disappointment that always hit when she thought about her dream. There was little chance it would ever be realized.

Ward caught her hand and met her gaze. "Jayme, you've impressed the hell out of me since you've been here. I can see that as an attainable goal for you."

"I thank you for that." She remembered the bitter disappointment of her father telling her that a woman had no place in a foreman's job. Ward's words validated her in a way she'd never felt before. The men she worked with seldom acknowledged her skill.

Ward got up and tended to the meat. The tantalizing odor of garlic-seasoned steaks filled the air. He closed the lid on the pit, and the sizzling sounds quieted as he strode toward the house.

Her eyes followed him, and she marveled at his powerful masculine grace. Was it being here, at his home, in his space, that made her so aware of him? She took a long draught of her iced tea, letting the cold liquid chill her from the inside out.

Ward came back, bringing a clean tray with him and laying it on the small table by the pit. Opening the lid, he added the potatoes around the edges of the grill. The intense aroma of cooking steaks filled the backyard again.

"You really know what you're doing." God, she was glad to be here tonight. Times like these had been so rare in her life. She'd missed so much, thanks to Blacke, and so had Dusty.

Ward grinned. "I've got a few secrets up my sleeve."

She narrowed her eyes. Where did he get that damn confident sexuality? The man wore it like a second skin.

He sat back down beside her and took a drink of his tea, then looked at her intently. "How are you doing?"

She froze. Did he know how attracted and confused she was? No, he couldn't. "Are you kidding me? Someone else is cooking dinner. I'm ecstatic."

He reached for her hand and twined his fingers through hers. "I'm glad you came. I hope you'll come again."

Something about holding Ward's hand soothed her. It was easy to be here with him. Her personal history said *beware—don't trust!* With him, though, her body sensed safety. She leaned back in her chair and sipped her tea as the day's tension slipped away.

When the meat was finally done, she brought out a bowl for the potatoes, and Ward loaded her up, then put the steaks on the tray. Her mouth watered at the tantalizing aroma of grass-fed T-bones hot off the grill.

Ward had already heated the green beans on the stove, and he brushed against her as they set their burdens on the cabinet. Tingles ran down her arm, and she glanced at him as he gazed down at her, eyes warm and open. He'd noticed the contact, too. She called Dusty away from his cartoons, and they filled their plates family-style right from the counter.

Dusty put his plate on the table. "Who's saying grace? I'm hungry."

She looked at Ward, then at her son. With no takers, she said, "Well, I'll say it. Grab hands."

When they were all seated, she began, "God, I thank You for allowing us all to be together tonight. Thank You for this wonderful food. And thank You for Mr. Ramsey. He gave me a job and a roof over our heads when we needed it desperately. I know that was Your doing, God. Thank You for keeping us safe. We love You, God. In Your Son, Jesus's, name. Amen."

Ward met her gaze and nodded. Smiling at the attraction in his eyes, she reached for the butter. Dusty chattered about the show he'd been watching, oblivious to the vibes on the other side of the table.

She took her first bite of tender steak and moaned, tilting her head back and closing her eyes. When she looked up, Ward's gaze was on her. "Hey, this is delicious. Cooked to perfection."

He grinned, hunger for more than food blazing in his eyes. "I'm glad you're enjoying yourself."

Her pulse thrummed from that look of his.

After another juicy bite, she said, "It's been a long time since I had a steak, and I can't remember a better one."

Dusty was having a hard time cutting his.

"Need some help, son?" she asked.

Ward got up. "Let me. Hang on there, young man." He took Dusty's knife and fork and cut his meat into small pieces.

Watching Ward cut up that steak went straight to her heart. Someone besides her caring for her son was such a unique sensation. It satisfied a longing she hadn't realized was in her. Is this what having a father for her child would feel like?

Dusty took a bite. "I love steak. I think this is the first time I've had it, right, mom?"

"Well, I think you had some at your grandpa's when you were little. You probably don't remember it."

"I won't forget this one. It tastes good."

She grimaced. How sad was it that her son grew up on cattle ranches, yet couldn't remember eating a steak? Mom fail number 10,391.

When they'd all eaten their fill, Jayme motioned to the cluttered table. "Dusty, you help me clear up. I'm doing the dishes. The cook gets to relax and enjoy himself now." She smiled at Ward and made shooing motions toward the back door. A little time without those flashing brown eyes of his would do her good.

The man appeared to have no problem with that. Grabbing a beer from the fridge, he headed for the backyard.

With Dusty's help, the table was cleared and the dishes were rinsed and in the dishwasher within a few minutes. Jayme's thoughts, however, were never far from the strikingly handsome man under the oak trees, which made it hard to follow Dusty's non-stop conversation.

He finally tugged on her apron. "Mom? Did you hear me?"

She wiped her hands on a dish towel and turned to him. "Sorry, honey. We're finished. Do you want to see more cartoons or go outside with Mr. Ramsey and me?"

The boy was torn. He dearly wanted to spend time with Ward, but the thrill of real TV was strong. He sighed. "I'll watch TV, I guess."

Following him into the living room, she made sure he found a show he liked. Once he was settled, she grabbed a beer and headed outside to join Ward, anticipation tickling her nerves.

Chapter Ten

The evening sky was aglow with the bright colors of the setting sun, and her pulse raced as she spied Ward under the trees.

Patting her chair, he beckoned her over. "Thanks for cleaning up. I have to admit I like the cooking much better."

"Don't we all." She eyed him as she walked over and sat down. Everything about this cowboy sent thrills rippling through her body. He was made to turn her on. With a twist, she removed the cap off her longneck and inhaled both the yeasty scent of the beer and the sweet evening air. This time was so different from the heat of the day. A little breeze puffed across the yard, and waterbirds called down at the pond.

Ward clasped her hand, his fingers lacing between hers. His was large, strong, and masculine, and hers slender and sturdy. They were a good match. He gently squeezed her hand. She looked up, meeting his gaze.

Lowering his head, he said, "I liked your prayer. You and Dusty are good at praying. I imagine God listens to you."

There was something melancholy about his voice. "I believe He does. In fact, I count on it. He's seen me through some tough times."

The dark curls at the nape of Ward's neck lifted in a passing breeze. Her gaze traveled over his shirt, picking out the muscles in his arms and the breadth of his chest. The energy that usually radiated from him was missing. Yeah, something was definitely going on.

Ward stared out over the pasture fence, rubbing his thumb across hers several times and sending chills up her arm. "I quit praying a long time ago."

She gripped his hand. *Oh, no. You poor man.* "You had cause." She couldn't imagine surviving what this man had. Would she still have faith if the Lord had allowed Dusty to be taken from her?

In the silence that followed, he squeezed her hand so softly she almost missed it, then sighed. "I've felt the loss from time to time. Of God."

With her other hand, she cupped his fingers. "I imagine." A stab of fear hit her. *Could I face life without my God?* It was a terrible thought. Poor man, he must feel so very alone.

He took a deep, slow breath and looked at her. "How's our boy doing in there?"

"He was mighty torn between spending time with you and watching those cartoons. I'm sorry to say you lost out."

Ward barked a laugh. "The story of my life."

She rolled her eyes. "Oh, right." A man this handsome didn't miss out on much.

He squeezed her fingers again.

The warmth of his hand was an anchor. No man had ever made her feel this way. His gentleness, his scent, and the rich, deep sound of his quiet voice gentled her.

"Tell me about your life. What's it like to be Jayme Bonner? Oh, and skip the part about coming to work for me. I know that sucked."

She threw her head back and laughed. "You're right. It did." She told him about the different places she'd worked, and some of the funny tricks the hands had pulled on her over the years. Being the only woman made her a target too hard to resist for many of the ranch hands. But in all save a few instances, it had been in fun.

"It's a nice life. It's what I've always wanted to do. I know my job is difficult for Dusty in some ways, though. But I'd die if I had to work inside all day long at Walmart or somewhere. And a miserable mom has a hard time raising a happy child; or so I think, anyway."

Ward slipped his arm around her shoulders and pulled her close. His earthy smell enveloped her. He held her hand in silence as the last wispy colors of sunset disappeared and the stars came out.

He kissed the top of her head. "Why don't we move inside, see what that boy's up to?"

He led her across the dark yard to the back door. The sound of the TV came from the other room as Ward grabbed them each a fresh beer and twisted the tops off.

Relaxed and feeling light as air, she smiled a little dreamily as she followed him into the living room.

Dusty lay sprawled in the recliner, half asleep and totally absorbed in his show.

Ward led her to the wide leather couch and urged her to slide in close to him. His broad shoulder and long arm comforted her as she nestled into his chest. It was so natural, as though she'd done it a million times before.

He brushed her curls back and kissed her forehead, then took her hand and spread it out on his knee. "Such strong hands. You know, they were one of the first things I noticed about you. Remember when we unloaded feed that first day? You grabbed those sacks from me and tossed them in a stack. I couldn't believe your strength."

She smiled to herself. *Yeah, and all the while you were scowling at me.*

He picked up her hand and held it, stroking back and forth with his thumb. It sent little shivers through her.

She squeezed his fingers. "When Noreen described you to me, I was expecting some old ogre. Then I saw this handsome cowboy working cattle, and I was completely surprised."

Ward laughed quietly. "Yeah, but then you met me, and it made sense."

"Uh-huh," she whispered.

He looked across the room. "I think someone fell asleep. Mind if I move him to the spare bedroom for now?"

She shook her head.

He got up and eased Dusty into his arms, cradling him gently as he carried him out of the room.

She stared after them. If there was ever a sweeter picture, she didn't know what it was.

Following a bathroom break, she came back into the room. Ward was already seated. She hesitated as she took in the sight of him—an arm slung across the back of the couch, one long leg extended, and a lazy grin. Her stomach contracted, and a rush of heat flooded her entire body. The guy was hot, sexy man personified, and he was waiting for her.

WARD'S EYES DRANK HER in. "Come over here, Jayme." His voice was gruff with suppressed emotion.

Excitement shot through him as she sank down next to him. Looking into her eyes, he saw anxiety and a hint of desire. *Baby, I'll take it slow.* He pulled her close and tilted her face to him. Lowering his mouth to hers, he feathered kisses across her irresistible lips, slipping his fingers through her hair and cupping her head. Heat rushed to his belly as he deepened the kiss, sweeping her mouth with his tongue. He kissed her in the sweet spot behind her ear, then slid his lips down her jawline, nibbling her neck. His heart thundered as he struggled with control. Her wildly drumming pulse hammered under his fingertips. *She's aroused now. Good.*

Surprising him, she initiated the next kiss, capturing his eager lips and making them her own, delving inside until he moaned hoarsely. *Hell yes, this is what I want.*

His chest tight as a bowstring, he panted, "Come here," and lifted her astride him. Holding her gaze, he clasped her hands, twining their fingers together as his heart hammered his ribs. He whispered, "You're beautiful, Jayme," and kissed the hollow of her throat.

She freed her hands, drawing him to her, kissing him possessively, covering every inch of his lips, leaning into him as if needing him to hold her.

I will, baby. I'll never let you go. He wrapped his arms around her waist, pulling her so tight he could feel the seam of her jeans on his belly. *Oh woman, you're everything I hoped for.*

Ward yanked her shirt out of her Wranglers and slid his hands inside, cupping her full breasts.

Locked in his gaze, her lips eased into a smile.

My God, you're lovely. He rubbed his thumbs across her breasts until her nipples pushed hard on the fabric of her bra.

She tossed her long hair back.

He laughed low and deep in his throat, his thoughts hazy, the blood pulsing in his temples. He kissed each luscious peak, using his teeth and leaving wet spots where her nipples were.

Arching back, she thrust her chest forward, increasing the pressure.

He ran his fingers up her back and then spanned her waist, his thumbs rubbing her belly as he kissed her between her breasts. *Jayme. Jayme. So precious.*

She slid her arms around him and kissed the top of his head before sighing deeply and pulling his hands into her lap. "It would be just my luck for Dusty to wake up and walk in on us. Having a child isn't too sexy." She sat up next to him again, tucking her shirt back into her jeans.

Ward growled like a bear and pulled her into him, kissing her quickly. "Honey, everything about you is sexy, don't you worry." Did he say sexy? She was female TNT.

"Time to take my boy home, I guess." Jayme patted his leg, and they stood. She smiled up at him. "Thank you so much for dinner." She laughed. "And everything else."

Pulling her into a tight embrace, he held her for a long moment. His heart still raced, and his body told him the night was young. Damn, it had been a long time since he'd been this turned on.

She hugged him back hard and kissed his cheek.

He said, "I'll bring Dusty to the truck."

JAYME LAY IN BED WITH her back to her son, reliving her time with Ward that evening. He'd opened himself tonight and let her in. It was magical, learning who he was. She'd never have guessed that sensitive man was inside her hard, gruff boss.

And who was she—this woman who let herself be cared about? Who let a man into her life? Everything was changing. She touched her lips, remembering their kisses. They were good changes. Yet, what if things went wrong? What then? God, it would hurt.

She chewed her lip. This was taking a chance. Not just for her, but for Dusty too. Keeping men out of her life had been safe—for both of them. If she moved forward, that safety would be gone. She squeezed her eyes shut. Tonight had been worth it. Knowing Ward was worth it. She sighed. It just was.

TUESDAY MORNING AFTER barn chores, Jayme headed in to cash her check. Yesterday they'd been on horseback all day, looking for missing cows in the rough terrain at the pasture near Rule, and she hadn't been able to get into town before the bank closed.

The old bank with its antique cowhide furnishings was quiet when she entered, the chill of the air conditioning cooling her arms. Only one of the two teller stations in the lobby was staffed. She glanced into the manager's office, and he nodded hello. Smiling, she waved and walked up to the teller. As she endorsed her check, one of the heavy oak front doors creaked open behind her.

A moment later a masculine voice boomed, "Put your hands in the air and stay still. Nobody touches any buttons, or I start shooting."

She froze. Ice shot through her veins like tiny knives. What would happen to Dusty if she were killed? God, she wanted Ward. Her knees went weak as she drew in a shaky breath, dropped the pen, and put her hands up.

Bootheels strode across the Saltillo tile floor and came up behind her. The teller's eyes were wide with fright. She glanced around, glimpsing a man holding a gun, before a hand grabbed her shoulder and shoved her forwards again, hard. Fear made her weakened legs stumble. "Give me your cell phone and get on the floor."

Heart thundering in her ears, she pulled her phone out of her back pocket with shaking hands and handed it over, then knelt and lay face down, thankful that her shirttail hid her own gun. She couldn't panic. After a deep, calming breath, she tried hard to remember what she had seen. A tall man, jeans, denim shirt tucked in, black gloves, black ski mask, piercing dark eyes. She moved her head so that the man came into her field of vision as he stood in front of the teller. Brown, square-toed western boots. Interesting. Was he a cowboy?

Behind her, a second man yelled at the bank manager, "Get out here, now! And lock that door."

Soon, the legs of the second man and the manager walked by her and stopped near the teller counter.

The first man said, "Mr. Manager, you go with my buddy here and open the cash vault while your employee gives me the money in her drawer. You understand what happens if we have a problem?"

She shifted her head slightly. The suit-clad legs shuffled and a voice answered, "Yes, I do."

"Great. Get going. Now."

Her heart sped like a quarter horse down a straight track. She hoped they had forgotten about her.

The first man said, "Open up your drawer. Give me the cash. Leave the bait money. I swear to God, if I find it later I'll kill you and your family. You get me, lady?"

A soft, high voice stammered, "Uh, y-yes. Yes."

A rustling sound came from in front of Jayme, along with footsteps. The booted man must have moved to get a better view. She heard the teller fumbling with the money, and coins clattered on the tile floor.

The man's voice growled. "Leave the damn coins. Shit."

A minute later, he barked at the teller, "Give me your cell phone."

There was more rustling.

"Okay, get over here with me, bitch."

He and the teller walked over, and the man kicked Jayme's hip. "Get your ass up. We're moving."

She rose to her feet, hip throbbing from the kick, heart beating crazily. *What now?*

The man motioned with his gun for both her and the teller to precede him to the door to the staff side of the bank. He pounded on it and, in a few seconds, the other man opened up.

As soon as they were inside, the first man told Jayme, "Lie down. Hands behind your back." He fastened her hands together with a zip tie.

Pain knifed through her wrists as the sharp plastic bit into her skin.

He tied her booted feet as well.

Next, he turned to the teller. "Lay down. Don't move." He performed the same operation on her as she cried out in pain.

When he'd finished, he called, "What the hell's taking so long?" and walked back to the vault.

The teller was crying softly. She didn't look to be more than nineteen or twenty.

Jayme smiled, using her eyes to encourage the young woman. "We'll be okay. We just stay still and let them do their thing."

Chewing her lip, she tried to think of anything else she might have learned. She'd seen the man tie up the teller. She closed her eyes and reviewed the scene in her mind. His jeans...they were Wranglers. She could tell by the cut and the pockets. She closed her eyes tighter. Yeah, that's right. The skin around his eyes was white. He was a white guy with dark eyes.

It made her feel less helpless to have a few facts to give the sheriff when they were discovered. They were *not* going to be shot today. She had a son to raise and, by God, she was going to do it.

Bootsteps sounded, and the first man's voice was loud again. "Keys. Show me the one for the door."

He must be talking to the manager. Keys jangled for a few seconds.

"Get on the floor with the others."

After the second man tied the manager up, both men stepped over her, and footsteps sounded as they ran for the front door.

Thank God. No one had been hurt. But now what? Her hands were going numb, and she had a stitch in her side from lying with her legs crossed.

The manager talked quietly with the teller.

Outside, a horn honked. A short time later, a female customer rapped on the counter and called, "Hello, hello, anyone here?"

The manager shouted, "We're in here. We've been robbed. Call the sheriff."

A few minutes later, a siren wailed outside. Jayme heard the doors open and the snapping sound of hurrying bootheels on the tile in the lobby.

The customer shouted, "They're in there, Sheriff."

The manager asked, "Sheri, where are your keys to this door?"

"In my purse. On a purple heart keychain."

The sheriff knocked on the door. "You in there, Bobby?"

The manager raised his voice. "Yeah, Connor. We're okay." He told him how to find the keys.

Footsteps walked away. In a few minutes, the sheriff was back, and keys rattled in the lock.

Jayme let out a sigh. The sheriff stood in the doorway, his deputy right behind him.

The sheriff shook his head. "Well, damn, what a mess. Just a minute." He told his deputy, "Get the snips for these ties from the car." With his hands on his hips, he reassured them. "You all hold on. The snips are easier on your wrists than a knife. We'll have you out of those things real quick." He craned his neck toward the vault, which stood wide open. "So they got the cash vault, too, Bobby?"

The manager sighed. "Yep, and one teller drawer. They were both armed."

The deputy showed up, and in a couple of minutes they were all standing in the lobby, rubbing their wrists.

She reached for her back pocket and her phone, then remembered that she didn't have it. The deputy noticed that she was armed. "You licensed to carry that?"

"Yes, sir."

"I guess the men who robbed the place didn't notice?"

She shook her head. "I was damned lucky. My shirt hid it."

He nodded. "Glad you didn't try to use it."

"No, sir. I have a son to raise."

The manager said urgently, "They took my keys, Sheriff. We'll need to rekey this place."

"Son of a—" The sheriff took off his hat. "I'll make sure we cover you until you can lock everything up tight. You better go call a locksmith. The rangers and the FBI should be here soon." He turned to Jayme. "I'm sorry, but you'll be here a good while. Do you need to make some phone calls?"

Her phone. Damn, it had all her numbers in it. She was at a loss. Then the manager spoke up.

"They left all our phones in the vault."

Jayme let out a long breath. Thank goodness.

The manager got Sheri's keys from the sheriff and went back to the vault to retrieve them.

She dialed Ward, suddenly glad that she'd hear his voice on the other end of the line. She needed the sense of safety he always provided. When he answered, she said, "I'm sorry I've been gone so long, boss." She went on to tell him what went down and added, "The sheriff says they're keeping me here for a while. I really am sorry about this."

"Oh, my God, honey. Are you okay?"

For the first time, she thought about how she felt. She'd had to face down a man who might well have killed her, for the second time in her life. She shivered. "I'm fine. I'll be better when they let me go home. I don't think it's a good idea to tell Dusty right now. I'll talk to him about it when I see him."

"No problem. Don't worry about being late, either. I'll look after Dusty when he gets off the bus. If there's anything you need, you just call me, you hear? We'll see you when you get home."

Five long hours later, the questioning was finished. She gave her description of the first man and went through her version of the robbery several times. By the time it was over, she was more exhausted than if she'd spent a full day on horseback.

The Texas Ranger who'd been the last to interview her accompanied her out the door. He shook her hand. "You make a pretty darn good eyewitness, Miss Bonner. Thanks for all your help."

She turned to make her way to her truck.

A man filming with a large video camera moved in.

A woman shoved a microphone in her face. "Can you tell me what you witnessed in the robbery, ma'am? What's your name? Did you recognize the suspects?"

The ranger's deep voice boomed, "She has no comment."

A man with a camera snapped her picture.

Jayme shook her head and hurried to her truck.

Sheriff's cruisers, FBI sedans and Ranger trucks were parked crazily around the block. Holy hell, this was a circus.

Weak from hunger and too tired to cook that night, she picked up fast food for dinner. That's when she realized that in all the mess she'd never cashed her check.

WARD WAITED FOR JAYME to get home while Dusty watched his cartoons. She could have been killed. And what about Dusty? That boy would be lost without his momma.

Today's robbery had shown him something clearly—Jayme and her son had worked their way into his heart, and he couldn't bear to lose them.

Running his hand through his hair, he gritted his teeth. By God, nothing would happen to them on his watch.

When Ward answered the door a short while later, Jayme looked done in. Her pale face and drawn eyes told the story of her experience. He pulled her into his embrace and held her close, kissing the top of her head. "Thank God you're safe."

She nodded her head, keeping her eyes closed.

He held her a moment longer, then eased her back and looked into her eyes. "How about I cook dinner and we relax tonight?"

With a wan smile, she said, "I stopped in town and grabbed all of us some burgers. I think I'll take my little man home and turn in early. Thanks so much, though, for offering, and for taking care of Dusty. Just, for everything..." She held his gaze with an obvious effort.

Pulling her into him again, he said, "That sounds like a plan. Rest is the best medicine for a crazy day like this one."

She pulled out his dinner, setting it on the table by the door while he helped the boy grab his backpack, and together they walked outside.

That night, as Ward watched the evening news from Dallas, he was shocked to see Jayme standing with a Texas Ranger in front of the bank in Howelton. She was identified by name as a witness to the robbery. Then the camera zoomed in on her face as a reporter tried to ask her questions. There was no mistaking who she was. Fear stabbed at him. The Dallas newscast was seen all over the northern half of Texas.

It seemed the robbery had made the big time because it appeared to be linked to a series of similar robberies around the state. The authorities were desperate for new leads.

He turned off the TV and sighed. If there was a better way to give away Jayme's location, he didn't know what it could be. He decided to keep the newscast to himself. He had a feeling there would be more bad news soon.

THURSDAY MORNING, WARD called Jayme, gave her a few instructions, and told her he'd meet up with her later on. He drove into town and stopped in at Allsup's. His worst fears were realized. On the newspaper stand, centered on the front page of the local weekly paper, was Jayme's photo. No one would mistake who she was; her name was written under it in bold letters. He scanned the article and swore under his breath as he took a copy up to the counter and paid for it.

He slapped the folded paper into his palm as he walked across the parking lot. There was nothing for it now. He had to tell her.

JAYME WAS MENDING FENCE at the back of the home pasture when Ward found her. Little butterflies tickled her belly as she saw her sexy boss driving toward her.

He pulled up along the cleared fence line and turned off the engine.

She wrapped Rowdy's reins around the barbed wire and walked over. "Howdy, boss."

He stepped out of the truck, his face tight with a frown.

Her heart started to pound. Was it Dusty? Had the school called him instead of her? She'd added him to the contact list weeks ago. She jerked her phone out of her pocket. No, she had four bars. She'd have gotten the call. "What? What is it? Is it Blacke?"

He reached out and clasped her arms, dropping the paper. "It's okay. I didn't mean to scare you. I have some worrisome information, is all. Tuesday night I watched the news, and you were on it, big as day." He went on to tell her the circumstances. "That's not all. I just got back from town." He picked up the paper. Opening it to the front page, he said, "Look at this. I read the article. It even says you work out here for me."

The blood drained from her face, leaving her light-headed in an instant. All the strength melted from her knees. She reached for Ward. "You don't understand. He has a pack of cousins in Dallas. A kid even came down and hung out with him on the ranch for a week. One of them is sure to see the news." Her life was slipping from bedrock to quicksand. The urge to run was overwhelming. Nowhere felt safe from the terror she knew was coming.

Ward put his arms around her. "You're not alone this time, Jayme. It'll be all right. I promise."

SATURDAY MORNING, WARD took Dusty with him into the Tractor Supply store where he needed to pick up a few things. He'd been wanting to spend time one-on-one with the boy, and Tractor Supply was a great place to wander around in.

The ride to Wichita Falls had been full of non-stop conversation. Ward remembered when Dusty's questions had made him nervous. Now he loved learning the way the boy's mind worked and teaching him about the world. He couldn't think of a word that described the way he felt when he was with Dusty. But it was good. Really good.

The store sold a little bit of everything: clothing, toys, trailer parts, hardware, feed, and vet supplies, to name just a few items. They weren't in a rush, so they walked up and down the aisles.

When they turned down the toy aisle, Dusty slowed to a stop. John Deere tractors, dump trucks, four-wheelers, and everything a young boy's heart desired filled those shelves.

Dusty ran his hand over a bright green tractor. "This looks just like yours, Mr. Ramsey."

"It surely does. Why don't you take that down and give it a closer look?"

The tractor was all metal, sturdy and heavy. Dusty touched the steering wheel, traced the tread on the tires, and examined the logo. "This is really awesome."

Ward had an overwhelming urge to give the boy a hug. He clutched the handle of the cart as unfamiliar emotions surged through him. "Why don't you put that in the basket? Every boy needs his own John Deere. In fact, I'm surprised you don't have one yet."

Dusty's jaw dropped as he stood transfixed.

"Well, go on, boy. Put it in the cart."

Dusty lowered it inside, then walked around and wrapped his arms around Ward's waist. "I love you, Mr. Ramsey."

He patted the boy's back and patted it some more, swallowing hard and blinking back the tears that threatened to overflow. Now he knew the word he'd been missing earlier.

He knelt and took Dusty's head in his hands. "Son, I sure love you too."

Chapter Eleven

In the early morning hours, Ward paced the living room, bare-chested, his hair tousled madly from a terrible night's sleep. Nightmares about the accident awakened him again and again. Why were they back? He'd been free of them for years.

Acid tore at his guts. He'd had a son. His own flesh and blood. How could he love another boy when he'd let his own son die?

When he thought of Dusty loving him, a knife twisted in his heart. He didn't deserve his love—couldn't accept it. It could happen again. He could let the boy down. He could...kill him.

He clenched his fists and groaned, striding into the kitchen and breaking his most important rule. Pouring three fingers of Maker's Mark into a tumbler, he downed a long swallow.

He sucked in a strangled breath. Jayme. How had he let her get so close? He'd loved his wife with everything he had. He couldn't love another woman. Not after he'd let Elizabeth die.

Her face appeared before him as it had the morning she'd kissed him goodbye before driving off to Dallas. The picture bled into the awful mess he'd seen in the small morgue of the local hospital.

No, he would not let that happen again. He raised his glass, swallowing several times, gulping the expensive whiskey without tasting a drop.

He slammed the empty tumbler down on the counter. Things were going to change—and change big—around his place.

The next morning, by the time he'd dressed and drunk two cups of coffee, he'd had time to make a plan. He would do things differently. Working beside Jayme all day was out of the question.

WHEN WARD STRODE INTO the barn, Jayme turned from where she was forking the last of the hay into the stalls, eager to greet him.

Dark stubble marked his hard, angular jaw line as her boss addressed her in a stern voice. "You'll be mending fence at the pasture off Highway 266 today. It's been a long time since I've done it, so I'm sure it needs tending to bad. After you pick up Dusty this afternoon, stick around. You can start on the fence here at the Highway 283 pasture. When you get finished with the pasture you're headed to this morning, which will take a few weeks, I'll have you work on the fence up at the Highway 6 place."

She nodded and kept her mouth shut. What in the holy name of hell was going on? Something was terribly wrong. It had been ages since Ward had worn that look on his face or used that tone of voice with her. She clenched her teeth, surprised at how much it hurt to have that dark scowl turned in her direction again. Pulling in a deep slow breath, she turned away. What hurt more than anything was the betrayal. She'd trusted him with her feelings.

A little while later, she headed out the drive. These three fence jobs would take a couple of months, at least. Well, she knew what all this back-to-back fence work was all about. The man didn't want to work beside her anymore. Well, this chore suited her fine. She couldn't stand being around him, either, if he was back to being an asshole.

Just thinking that hurt like hell. She sucked on her lip and stared at the flat horizon. One day the man aroused her with a passion she didn't know existed, and the next thing she knew he was treating her like she had the plague. What had made him do this one-eighty toward her? No matter. It proved one thing to her loud and clear. She'd been right—no man could be trusted.

When she got to the large mesquite pasture, she parked her truck and horse trailer near the entrance and unloaded Rowdy. After pulling out a stack of baling wire from the bed, she tied it to the back of her saddle. With her wire cutters, a fence stretcher, and a pair of limb loppers, she and the horse started walking the fence line from the gate.

There was no breeze. The morning sun blazed down on her, sinking through her T-shirt and burning her skin. She untied the long-sleeved, blue denim shirt from around her waist and put it on, feeling immediately cooler. Yet the pain of the sun's heat had been almost welcome—a distraction from the misery of Ward's betrayal. Coming as it had with no warning, it was like a force of nature, destroying her spirit with no rhyme or reason.

As she prepared to make her first repair, she draped the long reins over Rowdy's neck. He stood relaxed, one hip slung lazily and his hoof balanced on its tip. His head hung low and his eyes were half closed. He slept under saddle as only a well-trained, bored horse could. If only he could lend her some of that peace.

Using the loppers, she trimmed small mesquite, prickly pear cactus, and cedar trees that sprouted up either in the fence or in a swath ten feet out from the wire, leaving a clear area to drive a truck along the fence line. The sun bore down hard on her. She lifted her hat, letting in some air to cool her head. Just why... Why? How had this happened? The man had always been inscrutable, but this? It was crazy.

The mindless job of fence mending allowed her to worry endlessly about the cause of Ward's abrupt change in attitude. Each dark look had struck deeper into her heart. It made her realize just how much she cared about him. Her shoulders drooped and her boots felt like anvils as she worked her way down the fence line.

At noon she stopped and searched for a mesquite tree to sit under and eat her lunch. Making sure no snakes were near, she sat and leaned back against the rough trunk, staring down at her hands. A small breeze came up and, combined with the shade, made her feel a bit cooler.

She'd lost something today, and it had left her all hollowed out. Ward's kindness and her feelings for him had filled her up in a way she'd never experienced before. She *wanted* now—a nameless, hungry want that made her angry. Her life had been just fine before he came into it. She and Dusty had been whole—a good whole that made her happy. She'd known better from the start; known that letting a man into her life would never end well.

And what about the danger they were in? Her tight neck and shoulder muscles were testament to the worry she carried with her. It was just a matter of time until Blacke tracked her down. The news coverage after the bank robbery had all but given her location away. He could find her so easily now. She shuddered and pulled in a shaky breath. She had to protect herself and Dusty. Was she truly safer here, standing to fight, than she would be on the run?

Food stuck in her throat. She had no appetite to make it go down. Packing her remaining lunch stuff in the saddle bags, she led Rowdy out of the cool shade and moved on down a little, looking over each foot of fence as she walked. She checked the time on her cell phone. In a few more hours, she'd get home and meet Dusty's bus.

She stared back along the fence line. The drive down the fence was clear, and the wire was stretched tight over the entire length behind her. Let that damn Ward find fault with this. With any luck, she wouldn't see him when she got back. She couldn't please him when he was in a mood like today's, and it hurt too much to be around him.

LATER THAT AFTERNOON, after she picked up Dusty, she brought him along with her to the 283 pasture, about half a mile from the barn. The boy sat in the truck with the doors open and got out his homework.

With Rowdy at her side, Jayme began mending fence, slowly working her way down the line. The hot afternoon sun beat down on her shoulders and back. Her eyes felt heavy and her muscles ached, which was unusual. Sleep had been scarce the night before, fear of Blacke keeping her awake. She stopped and took off her hat, wiping the sweat on her forehead. Worry still had a stranglehold on her. It wasn't doing her any good, and it sure wouldn't make dealing with her boss in his current mood any easier.

At quitting time, they headed back to the barn.

She made quick work of throwing cow cubes and hay to the barn cows and cubes to those in the pasture. As she and Dusty walked toward her truck, Ward drove in from the direction of the ranch house. Her belly tightened.

He stopped and looked them over, frowning. "You fed already?"

Dammit. He was still in a mood. Pressing her lips together, she answered shortly, "Yep."

"You've got your orders for tomorrow. You won't be seeing me in the morning." His brusque voice left no doubt that he didn't like speaking to her.

He swung the truck around and headed back to the house.

She gritted her teeth.

"Is something wrong with Mr. Ramsey, Mom? He looks sad again," Dusty asked.

Swallowing something nasty that popped into her head, she said, "I'm not sure, hon. Maybe we need to give him some time to sort things out."

He looked down at the dirt and scuffed a rock under his boot. "Okay."

She pressed her mouth into a hard line. It'd better not take too damn long.

Chapter Twelve

Two days later, Jayme threw her gloves into the dirt on the barn floor, her eyes blazing. "Are you kidding me? Rowdy throws a shoe, and you think you can chew me out like I'm some teenager? I won't take it. And I'll tell you something else. I won't take another dirty look, either. I won't take anything off your sorry ass anymore. I quit!" Her breathing harsh, she picked up her gloves, brushed past him, and strode to her truck.

She was trembling so hard she dropped the keys on the floorboard before she could start the engine. She would never—never—be treated that way again. Backing up in a hail of gravel, she sped down the road to the cabin, leaving a cloud of dust behind her.

First, she had to pack everything except what they needed for the night. Then she would drive up and meet Dusty's bus. She'd withdraw him from school in the morning on their way out of town. She drew in a deep breath, and the sharp, lancing pain of her decision swooped in with it.

A sob caught in her throat at the sure knowledge that she would never see Ward again. Why, oh why, had she let him in? Why had she trusted him? Why had she allowed herself to care for a man? She'd known it could only lead to heartbreak. How could she have been so stupid?

She slammed the heel of her hand on the steering wheel as she pulled up to the cabin. Her rule about men and the ranches she worked on was there for a reason, dammit! Throwing herself out of the truck, she stomped up the steps.

In the bedroom, she took off her socks and boots and looked around, figuring out what of their few possessions she could pack. Her eyes landed on Dusty's small cardboard toy box and the two mitts inside. Why had she accepted them? She and Dusty had tossed the ball just fine without them. Who did Ward think he was, deciding what her son needed? It was none of his damn business.

Her insides clenched as she fought back a sob, willing the tears not to come. Would she be able to forget Ward's tender arms around her, how his hands felt as they explored her breasts, his lips feathering kisses across her mouth? Losing those things hurt way down deep inside; hurt in a way she'd never experienced before—where no man had ever touched her before. How had this happened? *Why* had this happened? That was maybe the most hurtful thing of all. Why did Ward hate her again?

She lay down and dragged a pillow into her belly, holding it tight. A black, feral nothingness, the one that had had its claws in her since childhood, ate its way through her heart. Gritting her teeth, she took in a deep, slow breath. Her loss weighed down her limbs.

After a few minutes, she bit her lip, rising slowly to sit on the edge of the bed. She couldn't give in to this. She needed to be calm when she saw Dusty again.

Leaving would kill her boy. He was already feeling it. Ward hadn't so much as looked at her son all week. How dare he? The man breaking *her* heart was one thing, but hurting her boy? Acid burned the back of her throat as her stomach churned. Yes, it was time to get the hell out of here.

AT THREE-THIRTY, WHEN she picked up Dusty and came straight home, her boy knew something was up.

As she fixed him a snack in the kitchen, he kicked his foot against the leg of the chair next to him, the thumping sound matching the thudding of her heart.

"Mom, what's wrong? Something's wrong, isn't it?"

His worried little face was like a knife in her chest. "Yeah, it is, son. I quit my job and—"

Dusty interrupted her. "We can't leave. Mr. Ramsey—"

She needed to get this over with. She had to make him understand. "Honey, I did quit. I don't think Mr. Ramsey wants me here anymore. He's been really hard to work for this past week, just like he used to be, and today was the last straw."

Sitting down beside him, she tried to explain. "People need to work where they're respected, Dusty. Besides, now that my picture has been all over the place since the robbery, it might be a good idea to move on anyway."

Dusty's face crumpled, and he put his head down on his arms, tears rolling silently off his cheeks.

She bit down hard on her lip, her pulse racing. This was her fault. She'd let Ward in. As she stroked her son's soft curls, each teardrop burned its way into her heart.

WARD PACED FROM THE quiet living room to the kitchen and back as fast as his legs would take him, Skippy following worriedly at his heels. He'd driven like hell around two pastures today without finding a single one of the missing cows. And no wonder. He couldn't see anything except the hurt, angry look in Jayme's eyes when she'd dressed him down in the barn and walked out on him. She'd tugged at his heart and made him feel every bit the asshole he was. He ran his hand through his hair for the hundredth time. How had this happened? He hadn't meant for her to quit. He just couldn't stand to be around her anymore, was all.

She couldn't leave, not with Blacke after her. It wasn't safe. If Blacke got a hold of her, there was no telling what terrible things he'd do. Ward stopped in the middle of the floor and stared wildly around. What could he do? Everything was out of control.

Though it was late, he strode to the counter, grabbed his cell phone, and punched in a number.

A familiar voice soothed his battered heart. "Hey, what's up, buddy?"

"Casey, she's gone and quit."

"I'm coming over." The line went dead.

He sank down in his recliner and, for the first time in days, the tension eased out of his limbs.

Forty-five minutes later, he'd just finished his third tumbler of Maker's Mark of the night. His drinking rule had been broken a lot lately.

Casey walked in the door without knocking, and Ward poured him a drink.

"Thanks for coming." He shook his friend's hand and helped himself to a fourth glass of whiskey. He was starting to feel a buzz.

Casey nodded. "Of course. Now tell me. Why is Jayme leaving, or do I even need to ask?"

"You know why. I was an asshole again." He dropped into his recliner.

Casey sat on the couch, crossing his ankle over his knee and taking a swallow of whiskey. "I thought things were going pretty well with you two. What happened?"

Ward leaned his head back and closed his eyes, letting out a heavy sigh. "I've been having nightmares again—bad. Worst I've had in a long time. I don't know, I feel like I...like I'm going to..." He shook his head and furrowed his brow, looking helplessly at Casey.

"Going to what, buddy? What's the worst thing that could happen with this woman and her kid?"

Ward set his drink down, covering his face with his hands, his heart heavy as a ball of lead. "What if I screw it up?" Shoving to his feet, he started pacing again. "What if I kill them, too? I mean, it's not like I've changed. I'm still the same bastard. I still work this ranch hard. What's to say I won't make a wrong decision again? Get them killed?" His breath caught in his throat, and he turned to the window, shoving his hands in his pockets. He couldn't go through that again. Not with Jayme and Dusty.

Casey walked over and gripped his shoulder. "Ward, you didn't get them killed. It's time you believed that. You've lived that day over in your mind for ten years. Now you'll always put your family first."

Casey took a drink, the ice clinking against the glass. "Give yourself permission to love again. Elizabeth would have wanted you to be happy. The past ten years would break her heart. Just do it."

He slapped Ward on the back. "Now, eat some crow and get that woman back, bud."

JAYME'S HEART RATE rocketed as a loud pounding sounded at the front door. She checked her phone as she sat up—five-thirty in the morning. She jumped out of bed, and the cool air from the air conditioner raised goose bumps on her arms. Was Blacke here? Was the barn on fire? Were cattle out on the highway? She tiptoed into the living room and peeked through the window, letting out her breath. Ward was at her door. Turning on the light, she threw it open, frowning. "What's wrong?"

He stepped inside, backing her up, and reached for her hands. "Everything!"

She thrilled to the wild look in his eyes and the way he pulled her closer to him. Her pounding heart filled with warm fire. She'd seen that look on a man's face right before he kissed her.

Ward's gaze took a walk all over her body. She was dressed in her sleep clothes—a tank top and skin-tight exercise shorts. Nothing about her was hidden from him and, despite herself, she responded to his masculine body's magnetic pull.

Dusty slipped up to Ward's side. "Mr. Ramsey, how come you're here in the nighttime? Is something wrong?"

Ward knelt and wrapped the boy in a hug. Cupping Dusty's head in his large hand and nestling it against his chest, he said quietly, "Everything's all right now, son. I'm sorry I haven't had time for you the last few days. I'm going to make up for it, okay?"

Confused, Jayme leaned her hand against the wall to support her. What had happened? Why was Ward here, and why was he suddenly different? This made no sense at all.

Dusty pulled away. "Can we throw some balls?"

Ward smiled and chucked him under the chin. "Anything you want, buddy."

She steeled herself. Just because this man was charming and knew how to push all her buttons was no reason to fall into his arms. She had no idea what had been happening with him the past week, but his behavior wasn't something she would put up with.

As he stood and reached for Jayme's hands again, a line appeared between Ward's brows. "Jayme, please forgive me. I hurt you, disrespected you, and treated you in ways you never deserved."

The knot in her stomach eased as his heartfelt apology sunk in. His hands were warm and strong around hers. This was the Ward she'd come to know. She leaned a bit closer to him, looking into his intent, dark eyes, trying like hell to read his mind.

He brushed a lock of hair from her face, then cupped her cheek in his hand. "You've never given me anything but your very best, and you've put up with me and all my faults. I don't deserve to have a woman like you in my life."

His hand on her cheek made her want to lean into his chest, to feel his hard body against hers, yet she resisted. He still hadn't told her why he'd treated her like shit.

He reached for her hand again and stared down at the floor. "I realized last night why I've been pushing you all away." When he looked up, his whole heart was in his eyes. "I don't feel worthy of you." Taking a deep breath, he squeezed her hands harder. "I let my family down, and I lost them. I couldn't bear it if I did that to you and Dusty too."

All of this had been because he couldn't bear to hurt them? To lose them? That was it? Her heart unlocked.

Raising her hands to his chest, she leaned into him.

He looked into her eyes. "But I'm willing to try. I can't stand losing the two of you. I want you to stay. I *need* you to stay. Will you please stay with me, Jayme?"

A flood of emotions filled her. God had answered her unspoken prayer. Tears rolled down her cheeks as she wrapped her arms around his neck.

He pulled her in tight, and his body molded to hers.

She cupped his face, kissing him gently, and they held each other, letting the hurt fall away. She whispered in his ear, "I'll stay." Resting her head against his shoulder, though, she knew there was still one thing he'd taken that she couldn't promise him yet—her trust.

Chapter Thirteen

Thursday, stopped at the Main Street light, Jayme stared in shock at the black truck in the cross traffic as it moved farther away. Her heart jackhammered her chest wall as she grabbed the dash for support. Why hadn't he called? He'd meant it when he said she'd never see him coming.

Ward was on the phone with a buyer for one of his young, purebred Black Angus bulls. He hung up and turned to her. "Great. He'll be out next week to look—" His brows drew down in concern. "What is it? What's wrong?"

"B-Blacke. He drove by." Her head was spinning. She couldn't pull air into her lungs.

Ward's eyes widened in shock. "What? Where? Just now? Tell me!"

She told him about the truck. "Turn right at the light." Hands on the window, face pressed to the glass, she stared in the direction the truck had taken.

There were two cars ahead of them, and it took a few moments before the light turned green. Ward roared through the turn and gunned the motor, far exceeding the speed limit within a few seconds.

They both scoured the side streets for the truck, but neither of them saw it. After five minutes of frantic searching, they had to admit that Blacke was gone.

Then it hit her—Dusty! Turning to Ward, she clawed frantically at his arm. "We've got to get to Dusty. Now!"

Ward wheeled the truck around, then sped back toward Main Street and the school.

Every minute they were on the road seemed like an hour to Jayme. What if Blacke had found out about her son? What if he got to the school first? She unbuckled her gun belt as they drove.

Ward pulled up to the front door as Jayme jumped out.

She ran inside and straight to the office. "I'm here to pick up Dusty Bonner. He'll miss a few days of school."

The lady in the office checked her ID and gave her a visitor's pass as Jayme signed him out.

Racing down the halls, she stopped outside his classroom door and took a deep breath. As quietly as possible, she opened the door and pointed at Dusty.

His teacher nodded and waved.

Dusty saw her at the door.

She motioned for him to grab his backpack and come on.

Once he came to the door, she grabbed his hand and pulled him into a run. The classroom doors passed in a blur as she focused on the end of the hallway.

Dusty panted beside her. "You know, Mom, we're not supposed to run in the halls."

"It's okay just this one time. We're in a hurry."

A wave of warmth swept through her when she spotted Ward right where she'd left him. Thank God for her guardian angel and his strength.

He leaned over and shoved open their door.

Dusty climbed into the truck. "Hi, Mr. Ramsey. I didn't know you were here."

Ward smiled and reached out his hand. "Climb on over here, buddy, and fasten up that seat belt. I'm glad to see you, too."

They drove the back streets through town and out to the ranch.

The ticking time bomb in her heart would explode if she didn't protect her son. She couldn't keep her hands off him, patting his leg, wrapping her arm around his shoulders, kissing his cheek. Dusty probably thought she'd lost her mind. Maybe she had. She couldn't take much more of this.

They pulled up in front of the little cabin, and she handed the house key to her son. "You know how to open the door. Go on in and find yourself a snack, okay?"

Dusty looked back and forth uncertainly between Ward and his mom, and then nodded.

As her son walked up the porch steps, Ward reached out and took her hand. "It'll be all right. We'll call the sheriff, and they'll find the bastard. And we'll always be armed. We won't let our guard down. Not one bit. We'll get him if they don't."

She shook her head furiously. Trembling and breathing in gasps, she said, "No, no, I can't risk Dusty. It's too dangerous. You don't know Blacke. Look how fast he found me. He'll hurt my son. He'll kill me. He won't stop." Her head started spinning.

She pulled her hand away, clutching her belly, willing Ward to listen to her. "Please, you've got to believe me. We're not safe here." Blacke's vile face filled her head. Darkness closed off her vision. She thrust her head between her legs and whimpered.

"Dammit!" Ward jumped out of the truck and ran around to her side. He wrenched open the door and lifted her out.

Inside the cabin, Ward laid her on the couch and put a pillow under her feet. He covered her with the quilt and sat down beside her.

Cold and clammy, she faded in and out of awareness. She had to get Dusty to safety. Far, far away from Blacke. Far, far away...

Holding her hand, Ward gently stroked her forehead.

She opened her eyes.

Dusty stood next to the couch, his eyes big as saucers, biting his lip.

The house was silent. No one moved.

Fighting back dizziness, she used her free hand to motion her son closer. "Come here, honey. You scared?"

He nodded. "What's wrong, Momma?"

"Remember when you were little, and you saw that coyote in the yard and you thought he was a wolf? Remember how scared you were?"

"Uh-huh."

"Well, I just got real scared like that. Bet you didn't know grown-ups could do that, did you?" In normal families, it only happened in nightmares. Her poor boy.

He shook his head slowly. "No."

"Well, see there? You just learned something." Closing her eyes, she hoped he'd leave it at that.

"Momma?"

Damn. "Uh-huh?"

"Do we have wolves around here?"

She sighed, and then opened her eyes. "Honey, we don't have any wolves here. But remember the man I told you about who I sent to prison? He's here in town looking for me. For a little while I let myself be scared. But I'm not anymore." *Damned straight. I'm protecting my son.*

Dusty sank down beside her. "I'll take care of you, Momma."

"Thank you, son, but that's not your job. When you grow up, you'll have somebody to look out for. But not now, okay? *I'm* watching out for *you* for a few more years, and that's the way it's supposed to be."

Ward put his arm around the boy. "Hey, partner, do you think you could do me a big favor? Your momma and I need to talk. If I set up the TV in the bedroom and fix you a snack, could you stay in there and watch a movie?"

Dusty looked at his mom and nodded tentatively. "Sure I can, Mr. Ramsey."

She covered her face with her hands. Ward moved about the cabin, but little interrupted her frenzied thoughts. She had to make a plan. *Oh God, help me! No! I'm better than this. Better than him. Blacke is nothing but a skunk and a cattle thief. I have to think. I have to keep Dusty safe.*

Tears leaked from her eyes. When she removed her hands from her face, Ward was squatting next to the couch, watching her, his face twisted in a frown. Her heart eased a little. It meant so much to have him beside her now.

He lifted her so that he could sit down, and then settled her on his lap. Cradling her in his strong arms, he kissed her tenderly. "What can I do?"

Somehow she had to make him understand. She put her hands on his face and looked him in the eyes. "You can hear me. Dusty can't stay here. Blacke will find him. He'll hurt him. And when he finds me, he'll kill me." Letting go, she took a deep breath. "There's something I haven't told you."

Ward looked steadily at her and nodded.

"Blacke heard me in the ranch office back then, reporting him to the sheriff. I didn't know it. He shouldn't have been around the place that day."

Biting her lip, she steadied herself before going on. "He attacked me when I went down to the barn. He beat me and kicked me within an inch of my life."

Tears gathered in Ward's eyes.

"Then he raped me. He was out of control. Said he'd kill me. He said the same thing at his trial. Now he's here. The man *will* kill me if he finds me."

Ward ran his arm across his eyes. Hoarsely, he whispered, "I'm so sorry, honey. So sorry." He gritted his teeth, his face flushing a dark red. "I'll kill that bastard. You don't worry about a thing."

She clutched his hand. "No! That's the last thing I want! If you see him, don't antagonize him. Call the sheriff. Please, you've got to be safe!" Gasping for breath, she leaned her head into his shoulder. "We've all got to be safe."

Ward kissed her gently. "Hush now, I'll be safe. Don't worry about me, you hear?" He cuddled her into his chest and brushed a kiss across her forehead. Crooning softly, like he would to a child, he rocked her.

AS JAYME SLEPT, WARD digested her story. Not even the death of his wife and child had affected him this way. That had been a terrible accident. What had happened to Jayme was pure evil. It couldn't go unanswered. Each beat of his heart sent blazing heat racing through his veins, but his brain was ice-cold. He'd make a plan. A plan that would protect Dusty, protect Jayme, and obliterate Blacke from this earth.

When Jayme woke, he kissed her, drawing his eyebrows together. "How are you?"

She looked absolutely worn out. That freaking Blacke. He'd never wanted to kill a man before, but now he couldn't say that. He'd see Blacke dead before he let him get to Jayme or Dusty.

"Better. Thanks." She sat up, moving off his lap. "Bet your legs are asleep."

He grinned. "Worth it." And she was. He'd needed to hold her while she slept. It made him feel less helpless in the face of the threat the convict presented.

Jayme squeezed his hand. "Don't get mad. I have to get Dusty out of here. I'm calling my dad, and I'll take him there. Blacke won't think to look backwards. At least, I hope not." She ran her hand across her face. "That call's going to be awkward, seeing as how I haven't talked to my dad in over a year. We're not that close."

Ward wasn't sure about letting the boy out of his sight, but he could see that the idea had merit. "Okay, but we're both going." By her furrowed brow, he could tell she had something else to say.

Looking hard and steadily into his eyes, she said, "I'm coming back here. This is where Blacke is, and I'm done running."

Ward pulled her close. "Why don't you stay down there with your daddy? I'll come back here. The sheriff will handle it. Or I will." She stiffened in his arms.

Pushing him away, she said desperately, "Please, Ward. Stay out of it. You mustn't take him on. You know he's only gotten worse in prison."

Before he could say anything, she swung astride his lap and pulled his face close.

His heart raced, and the crotch of his jeans was suddenly too tight. He wrapped his arms around her.

Her urgent lips sought his, sending fire pumping through his veins. She nibbled on his neck, came back to his mouth, and delved deep.

His body responded, every nerve alive to her touch. He'd never stop needing her.

She kissed him hard, demanding his sizzling response, sucking his lip into her mouth, and then pulling back.

She whispered, "You have that to live for. Don't throw it away on trash like Blacke."

She'd rocked him. He couldn't think. He hugged her tight to his chest. Did she mean what he thought she did? Could she? He pulled her back and cupped her face in his hands. Tear-stained, puffy from crying, brave—her face was all those things. He said, "I'd never throw our future away."

She held his gaze, and in the silence, he agreed. "You and me together, then. We'll make a plan. You pack for Dusty while I call the sheriff."

THEY ARRIVED AT JAYME'S father's old-fashioned ranch house in the blackest part of the night. She'd called ahead, and he met them at the door. He eyed Ward intently, but it was too late for conversation. Jayme and Dusty took the guest bedroom, and Ward slept on the couch.

Tired from the drive, he took a long time to fall asleep, thoughts of Blacke running through his mind.

In the morning, he slept in, as did Jayme and Dusty.

Jayme's dad had gone down and checked on things with the hands, then had come back home and cooked a big breakfast for everybody. Afterward, the man insisted on driving them all around the ranch and showing off some of the new things they'd done in the years since Jayme had last been home.

Dusty sat next to his grandpa, getting reacquainted while his mom was still around.

Ward was pleased. Her dad seemed like an okay guy, if a little quiet. The boy should be fine. Ward had worried about that quite a bit on the drive down. Jayme's memories of growing up hadn't been happy ones.

Jayme's fidgeting and obvious anxiety prompted her dad to say, "Why don't you folks go on now? Dusty and I have lots we need to do. You call us and check in when you can."

She put on a bright face and gave her son a big hug and a kiss. "You mind your grandpa now, you hear? I love you."

While Ward was saying his goodbyes, she rushed out the door. This was harder for her than he'd hoped it would be. He knelt and gave Dusty a hug. "You be good for your grandpa now, okay?"

The boy hugged Ward hard, his eyes squeezed tight shut. "I will. When can I come home?"

"Soon, son. Don't you worry. Just have fun with your grandpa." Ward kissed Dusty's forehead and, with a last pat on his shoulder, strode out the door.

Jayme was in the truck, tears rolling down her face. Ward headed out of the drive and moved down the road a couple of miles before pulling over. Reaching across the seat, he took her hand. "First time you've been apart?"

Looking ready to fracture into a million pieces, she started bawling and covered her face.

How much more could this woman take? An overwhelming need to protect her clamped down on his heart. He got out of the truck and opened her door, pulling her into his arms and rocking her side to side. "It's okay honey. He'll be okay."

Sobbing, she said, "What if I'm not doing the right thing? What if Blacke comes back south? I won't be here. I've always protected my boy."

Stroking her back, soothing her, he said. "Hush, now. We'll take care of Blacke. He'll never get to Dusty." He held her until she calmed down, wanting more than anything to make this terrible situation better.

Pulling away from him, she wiped her face.

He offered her his handkerchief. "We'll get through this. Blacke isn't going to win."

She blew her nose. "It's not like me to fall apart the way I've been doing the last couple of days."

"You're allowed. Don't worry about it." Patting her leg, he shut the door.

Heading back down the road, his gut in turmoil, he focused on how much he owed this Blacke. And he'd pay him back in spades.

Glancing at Jayme, he saw her staring out the window, looking as lost and sad as any woman ever could. A tidal wave of emotion struck him. He loved her. This tough, hardworking young mother had stolen his heart. Clenching his fists on the steering wheel, he made a promise. Blacke would *not* win.

Now that Dusty wasn't in the truck, he could focus on making a plan. It couldn't be out-and-out murder. It had to be legal. That was the catch. But the problem wasn't impossible. After all, the bastard was coming to him. He smiled, but nobody would take him for happy.

HER MIND SLUGGISH AFTER her crying jag, Jayme watched the familiar mesquite trees and prickly pear cactus pass by her window. The earthy, slightly dusty smell of Ward's ranch truck soothed her senses. How would she ever have coped with leaving her son if Ward hadn't been with her? Her dad had seemed different this time, though. Like he'd mellowed; become more outgoing and talkative. He really appeared interested in Dusty too. Had the years they'd been apart made him appreciate his family? Whatever it was, she was glad for Dusty's sake. Surely it would make her son's visit easier. How long would he have to stay there? God, they *had* to beat Blacke at this terrible game of cat and mouse he was playing.

Sucking in a lungful of air, she tried to make sense of her situation. Everything had been perfect. She'd made mistakes, though. Hadn't moved far enough away, maybe. She didn't know. But she'd lost it all. No more feeling safe. No more feeling like a normal family.

She glanced at the man at the wheel. Nothing could happen to Ward. He'd suffered so much already. She touched his sleeve. "Thank you for coming with me. Do you need me to drive for a while? You drove the whole way yesterday, and we won't be getting in until three or four in the morning." Even the fabric of his shirt reassured her. Like him, it was simple, straightforward, nothing fancy. She could count on Ward to be like that.

He took her hand and held onto it, resting it on the seat. "I'm fine. It frees my mind to think." Squeezing her fingers, he said, "The first part of our plan is safety. I'd like you to move into the ranch house until this is over. No strings. I have a guest room. You okay with that?" His brown eyes, honest and open, questioned her.

A soul-deep trust for this man filled her. It was as if a gray veil fell from her eyes. Never had she trusted another human being so fully and completely. She nodded. More tears threatened, and she turned away before they could spill.

He squeezed her hand again, without letting go.

She clenched her other fingers into a fist. No matter what happened, no matter the cost, she would make sure Dusty and Ward stayed safe.

Chapter Fourteen

The next morning, Ward stared across the room as dawn's light kissed the photo of his family resting on the dresser. He remembered that day so well—they'd taken the picture at Christmas and given them as gifts that year. His love for Elizabeth and Caleb swelled in his heart, but this time there was something else. A wide-open space replaced the razor-sharp stone of guilt he'd borne so long. His soul was light, almost empty, without that stone. Finally, he could love his wife and son without terrible heartache. And, best of all, he could fill that space with someone new. There was room for Jayme and Dusty now.

LATE THAT MORNING, as Ward knocked on her door, Jayme opened her eyes, her gaze landing on the picture of Dusty she'd brought with her from the house. As always, a surge of love swept through her. Wondering how her son was getting along with her dad, she called, "Come in."

Ward walked over to the bed, waving a steaming cup under her nose. "Anybody need coffee?"

Sitting up against the headboard, she grinned and admired the way his lean hips filled out his Wranglers before taking the cup and blowing into it. An intense chemistry swirled between them. "This is nice. Thanks."

He smiled and sat on the edge of the bed.

His clean scent and that wonderful aftershave of his enveloped her, tingling her senses. She took a deep breath and leaned her head back.

He laid his hand on her knee, and desire rippled through her. This sexy man was every woman's fantasy. She laid her hand on his, wanting to touch him.

His clear brown eyes warmed her as he spoke. "I want to talk with the sheriff today. See what our options are. Then you and I need to put our heads together and come up with a plan."

Her body shifted gears, and she froze. *Oh God. Blacke. Focus. Focus.*

Ward furrowed his brows. "Jayme? You okay?"

Talk of making plans had shots of adrenaline flooding through her, and she shook her head. "I—"

"Come over here." He took her coffee and set it on the nightstand, pulling her into a hug. "We're safe as can be now. Nothing's getting into this house without Skippy letting us know, loud and clear."

He held her tight. When she pulled back and opened her eyes, he stared at her intently, then leaned in and gently kissed her under the eye and on her chin. "Jayme, when you told me about what happened to you, I realized what these scars on your face meant. I always knew you were strong, and now I know how brave you are."

Something remarkable had just happened. She closed her eyes and let the powerful sensation sink in. Ward's words and gentle lips had healed her scars like medicine and bandages never could, taking the last trace of Blacke away. She clutched his shirt, not wanting to let go so that the wonderful feeling would go on and on.

Tucking her hair behind her ear, he said, "I have to go into town. Casey's in the living room. I don't want you here by yourself. I won't be gone more than an hour, hour and a half. Stay inside with Casey until I get back. Please? We'll feed when I get home."

She pulled back and rolled her eyes. "Yes, boss."

He kissed her quickly and left.

She returned to her coffee. It was kind of weird having Casey as a bodyguard. She'd always been independent, not to mention on her own. But since the attack, she'd never felt quite safe. Where was Blacke? Her stomach clenched. Had he found where she lived yet? What would he do? For sure, he'd do something, and it would be terrible. She pulled the covers up to her chin. Safety had never been further away in the nine years since she put him in prison. This time she had Ward beside her, though. Her rock-hard stomach eased a little. She wasn't alone.

Two hours later, Ward walked in the front door, a bounce in his step.

Casey grinned and got up from the recliner. "Hey, buddy, everything go okay?"

Ward nodded and smiled like the cat who ate the canary. "Yep."

She looked from one to the other. "What's going on?"

Ward shook his head. "Nothing." He waved at Casey. "Thanks for babysitting. I appreciate you coming over."

Jayme scowled. "Babysitting!"

Casey laughed and headed for the door.

She shot her chin at Ward. "Bet those cows in the barn are calling you names, boss."

"You know they are. We'll head down there in a few minutes." He sat next to her on the couch and pulled out his cell phone. Dialing the sheriff, he asked him if there was any news. Silently, he listened for quite a while before speaking up. "Thanks, Connor. I appreciate you working this so hard. I moved Jayme into the ranch house until this thing blows over. Keep my phone number handy, and call me if anything comes up."

She clenched her hands together. "No luck, huh?"

He shook his head and told her about the sheriff's new strategy. "Yesterday, one of the deputies went to the three motels in town to find out if anyone recognized the guy. He dropped off flyers with Blacke's photo, along with the department's phone number. Blacke might be sleeping in his truck, but it's worth a shot."

Ward reached for her hand. "The other deputy stopped at all the gas stations and cafés and handed out flyers. Everyone was asked to call if he shows up."

He shrugged. "Maybe someone's seen him around. He's got to be somewhere. He has to eat, sleep, and buy gas. They'll find him."

He pulled her close. "We'll get through this."

Sighing, she nodded. "Yup, I know we will." She breathed in his smell and closed her eyes. His arms snuggled her, and she could feel each of his fingers pressing gently into her back. He kissed the top of her head tenderly. This man made her feel absolutely safe.

He stood and helped her to her feet. "How would you feel if we told Casey and Annie about our troubles? I think having them in on this would help. All I told Casey today was that I didn't want you staying alone. I know he's curious as hell. I figured it was up to you whether you shared your story or not."

The first thing she wanted to say was no. She was used to handling her own problems. But then she changed her mind. "It might be good to talk to Annie." Though she'd never had a girlfriend to share her life with, Annie was someone she'd come to feel especially close to.

"Great, I was hoping you'd say that."

Ward made the call. "Hey, Annie, how are you?" He listened for a few seconds. "Well, good. I was wondering if you all might be up for some company in a couple of hours. Jayme and I would like to drop by." He paused as Annie replied. "Oh, now, don't go to any trouble. We won't stay long. We just want to visit for a few minutes." Nodding, he said, "Okay, we'll see you in a little while."

He grinned. "Oh, you know she'll be dying of curiosity until we get there. That Annie." Shaking his head, he reached over and grasped her hand.

Is this what a normal life felt like? Having a partner to take care of you? Friends to share your problems with? She'd missed out on so much thanks to that damn Blacke and how his attack had affected her.

JAYME LOOKED OVER AT Ward as they pulled into the drive at Casey's house, glad of his solid strength beside her.

He smiled encouragement as he turned the truck off.

She wanted to do this right—stay calm, keep it impersonal. Talking about it was easier that way.

Annie answered their knock, and the first thing she did was smother Jayme in a hug and turn to Ward. "Come on in, you big lug." She gave him a hug, too, and then wrinkled her brow. "Lord, Ward, a gun?"

He nodded, pressing his lips together, and followed her inside.

Jayme blew out an anxious breath. She'd left her gun at home since Ward had his and she'd be talking about something so emotionally draining today. She found that she missed its solid weight on her hip. She felt as if having it on would somehow give her more courage to talk about the attack.

Annie brought them into the living room. "Sit down, you two. Casey will be in here in a minute. I'll be right back. I'm warning the kids that this is officially a grown-up zone."

Ward led Jayme to the couch. She sat down while he took off his gun and laid it on the coffee table. The room showed Annie's warm, happy personality. Soft, natural colors welcomed them, and a couple of quirky signs reflected Annie to a T. The scent of homemade bread baking wafted from the kitchen. Jayme leaned back into the cushions, relaxing a little. That's what Annie did to her—made her feel comfortable.

Ward sat next to her and held her hand. "Nervous?"

She shook her head. "Not too bad. I never like talking about it, but if I had to choose, it would be to Annie."

He tugged on her hand, and she moved closer as he slid his arm around her shoulders. Warmth snaked its way through her belly, and some more of her tension eased. This man's chest was made to cuddle her. He fit her perfectly. She breathed in his scent and relaxed. Maybe talking today wouldn't be so bad. Not with Annie and Ward with her.

Casey walked in—and did a double take.

Ward laughed. "Yes?"

Casey grinned. "Well, I'll be damned. You two want a beer?"

Ward grinned wider than Casey. "Sure."

She rolled her eyes. *Guys.* And that Casey—he loved teasing Ward.

Annie walked in. Too classy to do a double take at the sight of them snuggled together on the couch, her eyes just got round. "Casey already offer you two something to drink?"

Ward gave a thumbs up. "Yep."

Jayme bobbed her head.

Annie sat down, hands folded in her lap and an expectant look on her face.

Casey came back in and handed them each a beer. "Well, let's get this show on the road." The teasing grin had never left his face. "You have something to talk about, buddy?"

Jayme looked from Casey to Ward. What on earth was going on here? He was teasing Ward—but about what?

Ward cracked up. "Later, you." Then he got serious. "Jayme and I have a problem we want to share with you all." He turned to Jayme. "Do you want to do this, or should I?"

With Ward solidly by her side, she filled them in on the situation. It wasn't so hard to talk about, not after she got started. The empathy in Annie's eyes gave her the courage to make it through to the end.

"Oh, honey." Annie moved over to the couch and clasped her hand.

Jayme continued. "He beat me so severely I was in the hospital for a week. And now he's here in Howelton."

Annie gasped. "My God, can't the sheriff do anything about him? This is crazy."

Ward tapped his fingers on his knee. "We're working with Connor. He's doing everything he can. And Jayme and I are going armed." Nodding toward the gun, he said, "He's a nasty son of a bitch, and I don't put anything past him."

"Where's Dusty?" Casey asked.

Jayme rubbed her palms up and down her thighs. The question brought a rush of anxiety with it. "I took him south to my dad. But what if Blacke—that's the bastard's name—finds him?" She tried to fill her lungs, but there wasn't enough air in the room. She tried again, but couldn't get enough. Clenching her fists, she opened her mouth wide and sucked in hard.

Ward clasped her shoulders and gave her a little shake. "Honey, it's okay. Just breathe slowly now. Don't take such big breaths. You'll hyperventilate."

She pinched her lips shut and breathed through her nose. Panic threatened to overwhelm her as she took small, shallow breaths.

Ward rubbed her back and murmured reassurances to her.

Annie knelt in front of her, patting her knees.

God, could she look more idiotic? She held her breath and counted to ten, closing her eyes and thinking of Dusty. *He's okay, he's safe. He's safe with my dad.* The pressure on her chest eased. She could breathe more normally now. She opened her eyes and blinked.

Ward's worried gaze met hers. "You okay, honey?"

She nodded. "Better. Sorry, I just lost it. You know, is Dusty safe, and all."

Annie patted her leg. "Now, honey, far away from here is the best place for that boy. You did the right thing taking him down south." She moved back to her chair. "We're with you two. Whatever you need."

Casey nodded emphatically. "Hell yes, we are. Ward, I've got your back. You tell me the time and place. I'm there, buddy."

She shook her head. "No, wait. I don't want you two involved. This is too dangerous. I was only hoping for moral support." Her hands trembled. She couldn't put these sweet people in Blacke's sights.

Ward reached over and covered her shaking hands with his large, tanned one, smiling reassurance.

She gripped his fingers, drawing strength from her guardian angel. "Could you just let us talk things over with you? It's wonderful to be here, to share the burden with you. That's really all we need."

Annie turned to Casey, and a look passed between them. "Jayme, you can have anything you want. We're here for you."

Ward pulled her in close. "Jayme's staying at the ranch house with me right now. It's too dangerous for her to be down at the cabin by herself." He looked from Annie to Casey and smiled. "I guess you realize about now she's more than my cowhand."

Casey cracked up. "You don't say."

Jayme sighed loudly and shook her head, looking over at Annie. These two guys had something going on between them. That Casey was such a tease.

"Jayme, don't you listen to a word those two say. Come with me. Would you like some coffee? And I have some chocolate chip cookies I made yesterday."

"Please." Never had an invitation been more welcome.

The kitchen, done in leaf green and gold, was inviting and cozy, just like Annie. Jayme sat down on a stool at the island while her friend made coffee and kept a steady stream of conversation going. As Jayme listened to Annie's prattle, knots of anxiety dissolved one by one. Having a best friend was a source of comfort like no other.

Annie set two steaming cups on the colorful, Mexican-tiled island top and a plate of cookies between them. "So, how are you holding up, honey?"

She stared into her coffee. "I think I'm losing my mind. My emotions are out of control. I'm crying one minute and having crazy thoughts the next. And"—she looked up into Annie's eyes—"I'm worried about what will happen to Dusty if Blacke gets to me. All this—carrying guns, and the sheriff and his deputies looking for him—well, that's just fine. But Blacke's sneaky and the meanest creature God ever put on this earth. I know he can get around our protections. And I'm all my son has. I can't bear the thought of my daddy raising my boy. I don't want the life I had for Dusty." Hot tears rolled down her face as she raised a shaking hand to wipe them off. Annie couldn't know what it was like, growing up without love. Life was almost not worth living. There were times when she'd wanted to die.

Annie slipped her arm around her. "Listen, you're not alone in this anymore, honey. All of us are going to be looking after you. That rotten man doesn't stand a chance. Don't let him into your head like this. And Ward? Let's just say they don't come any tougher than that man. If I was in trouble, he's the guy I'd want on my side." She kissed Jayme's cheek. "You wait and see. It'll all come out right."

Annie handed her a cookie, put her coffee cup in her hand, and talked about her kids until Jayme relaxed.

Speaking with Casey and Annie had been a release. Ward was right. Sharing her problem was what she'd needed to do. She was battle-ready now. Blacke had better look out.

Annie set her mug down. "We'd better get on in there with the boys. They're bound to be wondering what we're doing in here. And, besides, if I leave Casey alone for five minutes, there's no telling the trouble that man will get up to."

When Jayme walked into the living room, Ward and Casey were standing, heads together, over by the window. Ward thrust something into his pocket.

Casey grinned. "Well, it's about time, girls."

"Oh, hush. I'm sure you two kept busy gossiping," Annie retorted as she headed to her chair.

Casey glanced at Ward, grinning even wider. "Oh, that we did. That we did."

Jayme eyed the two. The guys were definitely up to something, all right.

Ward laughed and shook his head, walking over to the couch and holding his hand out to her. She sat down next to him, and he wrapped his arm around her, snuggling her up close. She leaned her head into his shoulder, and his wonderful scent filled her head. Her body responded. The fabric of her bra was suddenly too rough, pressing against her sensitive nipples.

With the weight of fear gone, her body was ready and willing to respond to this tender, sexy man.

She realized Annie had been talking and tuned in.

"I'm so glad you two came over." Annie's expression hardened. "But I'm worried about this crazy mess going on. I'll be praying that the sheriff finds this creep and puts him in jail." She pointed at Ward. "More than anything, though, I'm happy to see you're getting over being an ass."

Ward cracked up.

"Here, here." Jayme pumped her fist.

Ward shook her shoulders. "Hey, you."

She loved it that he could laugh and tease. "Annie, your friendship means so much to me. Thanks for everything."

Ward patted her leg. "You ready to go?"

He strapped on his gun as Annie walked her to the door. Sweet emotions whirled inside her. Freedom from fear, new best friends, and a man who cared for her—life was incredibly sweet today.

Annie hugged her and whispered in her ear, "I'm so happy for you. You deserve a man like Ward."

To her surprise, Casey gave her a hug, too. "You come back anytime. You don't need to bring this old fart along, either. You're always welcome here."

"Hey," Ward complained.

She grinned. "Thanks, Casey. I'll remember that."

As they drove the road home, she held Ward's hand fiercely. Blacke was out there somewhere, and he was on the hunt.

Chapter Fifteen

Late that afternoon, Jayme glanced across the truck at Ward. A smiled played across his lips as he sat relaxed, fingers laced through hers.

As she gazed at his strong, handsome profile, she realized that this hardworking, sometimes contrary man had stolen her heart. The corners of her mouth curled up. Nobody who knew her would believe that Jayme Bonner had fallen in love. She hugged her secret close, the newness of her glorious discovery thrilling her.

They were headed out on Highway 277 toward Stamford and the Walmart there. Ward wanted to lay in supplies so that they could keep to the homeplace and the safety of the thick, adobe walls of the ranch house. She leaned her head back against the seat and relaxed, basking in the warmth of her newfound love. More than ever, she was committed to making sure Blacke didn't come near Ward or Dusty. She squeezed Ward's hand, wishing they were already home so that she could show him how much he meant to her.

He grinned and squeezed back, then glanced in the rearview mirror.

She looked over her shoulder.

A black truck surged past them.

Ice shot through her veins as she shouted, "Bla—"

A loud boom cracked through the air.

Her head slammed violently into the side window. Her vision went black.

Ward's truck careened off the road and down an embankment.

She screamed, bracing on the dash, as the truck smashed into a mesquite tree.

Ward yelled out in pain as the truck rocked to a stop.

Blood poured out of a gash on the side of her head, and dizziness sent nausea slithering to her stomach.

Slowly, she raised her head. The dash and door were caved in on Ward's side of the truck.

"Are you hurt? What's wrong?" She yanked on her seat belt, but the latch was stuck. She pushed again and again on the button and pulled with all her might on the strap, and it came loose. She moved over next to Ward.

He was hauling on his left leg, in obvious pain. "It's jammed bad. Some bastard ran us off the road." He narrowed his eyes and peered at her. "And you're bleeding. Let me see."

She thrust his hand away. "It's not a problem." *God, Blacke. He's done this. Where is he? We need help.* She looked for her cell phone, but it was missing from the dash console where she always set it. Scooting over, she stepped out her door, intending to search the floorboard for it. Movement up on the highway caught her attention.

Dirk Blacke's truck was pulled over on the shoulder. As she watched, Blacke rounded the front of his truck with a gun in his hand.

She gasped and looked around desperately for cover. She flipped the loop off the hammer of her gun. Adrenaline raced through her body.

Just then, a blue Dodge Ram pickup pulled up, parking behind Blacke's truck. The woman in the passenger side got out.

Blacke glanced at her, backed up, turned, and paced around the front of his truck, yanking open the driver's door.

Jayme yelled, "Call 911. We need an ambulance and the sheriff."

The woman waved and returned to her truck as Blacke's tires spun in the gravel, throwing pebbles back at the blue pickup.

The Ram's driver leaned on his horn.

As Blacke sped off down the highway, Jayme tried to get his license plate, but he was too far away.

Crouching down on the floorboard to get a look at what was going on with Ward's leg, she explained that Blacke had been the one who ran them off the road. Her system was still flooded with adrenaline as she inspected the wreckage under the dash, scrabbling through it until she found her cell phone.

Ward slammed his fist into the steering wheel. "Dammit! Forget about me. Pull your gun and keep an eye out. And for God's sake, come here. We need to do something about your head." He laid his revolver next to him on the seat.

"In just a minute." She had to find out what was causing the bleeding in his leg. There was a lot of blood, and his leg was stuck inside the mangled metal.

Sweat beaded his forehead, and his face was pale. She kept the information about the blood to herself. No need to get him even more worked up. Easing backward, she grabbed a wad of napkins from the passenger door panel and pulled a flashlight out of the glove box. She couldn't get to the source of the bleeding, though, so she backed out again.

Ward motioned her over to him. "Turn around. Let me see that."

He took the napkins from her and gently dabbed around her head wound. "It's still bleeding hard."

Wincing, she bit her lip as he worked on it. There was no sign of Blacke coming back yet.

"Hold still. I'm applying pressure. Turn your head a little so you can keep an eye on the road."

His hands were shaking, and she hoped he didn't go into shock. His gentle fingers reassured her. Ward was her rock and, despite his injury, she felt safe with him.

Meanwhile, the good Samaritans in the blue truck had come down to check on them. The woman took over holding pressure on Jayme's head while the driver went back up to the road to flag down emergency vehicles.

Jayme, standing by the passenger door, kept one eye on the road for the black truck and the other on Ward as he became increasingly pale and drawn from the pain. Eventually, the wail of the ambulance signaled the arrival of help. The napkins on her wound were saturated, and blood was dripping down her neck and onto her shirt. She didn't want to think about what the floorboard under Ward's leg must look like. Her fear for him didn't help the bleeding from her head, either.

Ward hadn't said a word in several minutes. Was he going into shock? Her pulse raced, which wasn't good for her head. *God, let us both be okay.*

The EMTs hurried down the incline toward the truck.

Her hands clenched into fists. She had failed. Blacke had gotten to Ward.

JAYME SAT IN THE ER room in Abilene, the acrid hospital smells strong in her nose. Her chair was crammed next to Ward's bed. She stared through the open curtain, running a jerky hand through her hair. The sheriff had been and gone long ago. She'd explained their situation and given a description of the truck, asking him to contact the Haskell County Sheriff's Office for more information about Blacke.

Ward was in a lot of pain, and she knew he was scared about how he would manage the ranch with a broken leg. As if nausea from her head trauma wasn't enough, her failure to protect him literally made her want to throw up. She had to figure out a game plan. Time had run out.

She'd called Annie and told her what happened. Her friend had insisted that she and Casey would drive down and take them home. The two were out in the waiting room now.

Midnight had come and gone before Ward was released. He had a fractured tibia, but he wouldn't need surgery. After a dose of IV antibiotics and a tetanus shot, his leg had taken thirty-seven stitches.

Her head ached as she followed Ward's wheelchair out to the waiting room. The truck window had given her a hell of a whack. She had a large knot on the right side of her head, and her face was swollen. The cut had cost her thirteen stitches and her own tetanus shot.

Casey and Annie had brought hamburgers with them, but Jayme couldn't eat. When they left the hospital, they went by and filled their prescriptions at an all-night pharmacy. After that, all she wanted to do was get home. They still didn't have groceries, though. Everything was a mess.

The guys rode in the front of the SUV, their quiet conversation about the accident something she didn't want to hear. When they were finally on the highway heading out of town, she leaned her head back and closed her eyes.

Annie reached out and patted her leg. "Honey, I'm scared for you. I mean, I believed you two when you told us about the guy, but this is awful. He meant to kill you—shoot you while you were helpless. Who does that?"

Jayme clenched her fists and stared at her friend. "A sorry son of a bitch, that's who. A low-down, cowardly bastard." All the anger she'd suppressed since the accident came boiling to the surface.

She was more certain now than ever. "I can't let Ward get hurt again. I can't."

Annie raised her eyebrows. "Well, honey, I don't see—"

"No, I mean it. This isn't his fight. He's collateral damage. Blacke wants me." That bastard would do anything, hurt anyone, to get to her. There was no end to the malevolence in him.

Annie squeezed her hand. "Don't you go worrying about Ward. That man can take care of himself."

She shook her head. It was no use. Annie didn't understand. She'd never witnessed the evil in Blacke. She didn't realize the lengths he would go. Jayme had experienced the darkness in his soul, and she wasn't about to let that malice touch Ward again.

By the time they'd reached the ranch house, she'd made a plan.

Chapter Sixteen

Ward swung himself unsteadily on his crutches, following the sidewalk to the front door. For the first time in his life, he was physically helpless. When Jayme needed him most, he could only hobble around. How had he lost control of the truck? And surely there had been a way to avoid hitting that tree? The similarity to the accident ten years ago was not lost on him.

The taillights of Annie's SUV disappeared down the drive as Jayme unlocked the door. Flipping on the porch light, she turned to help Ward over the high threshold.

"I got this, dammit," he snapped, then gusted out a breath. *Way to go, Ace. Why don't you kick a puppy, too, while you're at it?*

Jayme jerked her head back in surprise.

He grimaced. "I'm sorry. I'm just so damned mad about all this, I could spit."

She frowned, shaking her head, nearly in tears. "I'm so sorry you're hurt. This is impossible. Blacke can pick his place and time to come after us now."

"Let's get out of the doorway. Hell, let's just go to bed. I'm worn out." If the man had been following them, it stood to reason he knew where they lived. God, how was he going to protect her now?

Jayme let Skippy inside from the backyard as Ward headed down the hallway. Jarring pain shot through him with every movement of his leg. The pills had to help. No way would he be able to keep Jayme safe feeling like this. He sat down on the bed and unbuttoned his shirt. His whole body hurt. His jeans had been cut off, but Casey had brought him a pair of baggy cargo shorts to wear home. His cast reached to mid-thigh on his left leg and, of course, he couldn't bend his knee.

He hiked himself up with his right leg and slid his shorts down, then sat down again. *This shit is hell.* He pulled his shorts lower, then used his right foot to drag them off his cast. *Dammit, that hurt! What a pain in the ass.*

He was scowling when Jayme came into the room.

She took one look and said, "Maybe these pills will help. You get to take two the first time."

The woman appeared absolutely worn out. He worked at it and found a pleasant expression for his face. No way was he going to take his frustration out on her. "Thanks. I think I might be going back on that asshole thing I promised."

She laughed and bent down to kiss him on the cheek. "I'll ignore it if you do. Let's get you to the bathroom."

While he brushed his teeth, he had one thought—Jayme could have been killed today. Veins pulsed in his temple. Blacke had come so close. If those people hadn't pulled up, they might both be dead. Fear slammed into him. It could still happen. Tonight, while they slept. He couldn't get out of bed fast enough to counter an attack.

He splashed cold water on his face and dried it off. The sheriff and his deputies would scour the county tomorrow. They knew what the bastard drove, and his ride was banged up now, making it that much easier to recognize. If they made it through the night, Ward's job would be to hunker down and keep Jayme safe. This house was a fortress. The more time they spent here, the safer they'd be.

Jayme waited by his bedside. All he wanted to do was protect her. Leaning his crutches against the wall and standing on one leg, he wrapped his arms around her. What would his life be like now if the worst had happened? He shuddered and rested his cheek on top of her head.

She pulled back. "Let's get you into bed. I know you're exhausted."

He cupped her face in his hands and brushed a slow kiss across her soft, full lips, more determined than ever that nothing and no one in this world would hurt her. He sat on the bed, and she gently lifted his leg up as he lay back on the pillow.

She snuggled the covers all around him and kissed his cheek. "Close your eyes and relax. I'll be back in a few minutes."

He reached for her hand. "Hey, don't take this wrong, but I want you to sleep in here tonight. If Blacke breaks in, I can't get up and protect you. I need you beside me and my gun. Bring yours in here, too. This is where we'll make our stand tonight. Will you do that for me?"

She looked at him a long moment, then nodded.

He watched her go, a steel band clenching his chest. He glanced at the bedside table. Jayme had put both guns in her purse before they took the ambulance ride. His .38 lay ready. But the bastard would already be in the house and at the bedroom door before he could use it. He wasn't just afraid... He was scared shitless.

JAYME SLIPPED INTO her room and shut the door, leaning against it. Ward was so helpless. There was no way he was a match for Blacke in this condition. It was all her fault. If she'd kept on going down the road that day, instead of asking Ward for a job, he'd be safe. It was on her now. One way or another, she'd finish this.

Grabbing her bag, she stuffed her toiletries, clothes, and purse inside it, then went back to the master bedroom.

Ward opened his eyes as she lay down on the bed beside him and covered herself with the quilt she'd brought from the couch.

"Turn out the light, will you?" she said softly.

He reached over and switched off the lamp.

Snuggling into his warm, powerful chest, she was careful not to jostle him.

He slid his arm around her and pulled her close, kissing her forehead.

She had to tell him how she felt. She wanted him to know how much he meant to her. Then, tomorrow, he'd understand. "Ward?"

"Yeah, honey?"

"I was so scared for you when Blacke was coming with his gun. I couldn't bear it if—"

"Sweetheart, you don't need to be afraid for me. My God, I have to keep you safe. I—"

No, she must get this out. She stilled his lips with her fingers. "Let me say this. Please." She took a deep breath, needing a few seconds to pull her thoughts together.

"I've lived my life alone, except for Dusty. That was okay until I met you. You showed me what was missing; what having a good man in my life can mean. Ward, I owe you more than I have words for. I care so much for you—"

Ward held her face and kissed her thoroughly, his passion almost bruising her sensitive lips.

God, how she loved this man. Rising, she answered him with desire of her own, capturing his mouth, delving deeply with her tongue. She feathered kisses along his chiseled jaw and nibbled his earlobe, his throat. Finally, she eased back, taking in a breath. She never wanted to live without him. That's why this night was necessary.

He brushed her hair back. "Jayme, I never thought I'd care again. I didn't know I could." He pulled her into him and held her tight. "That boy of yours. He's something. He's like my son would be, if he had lived. I'd like to think that, anyway. I guess you know he's stolen my heart."

Tears seeped from her eyes. This man. This good, good man. She had to protect him. *Please God, keep that bastard Blacke away.* Leaving Ward would be the hardest thing she'd ever do.

Laying her head on his chest again, she slid her fingertips back and forth, back and forth across his brow. "Hush, now. I want you to sleep. We both have things to face tomorrow."

THE FIRST THING JAYME did when she got in her truck was check Google and make hotel reservations in Altus, Oklahoma. Fearing that any minute Ward would wake and find her gone, she slipped quietly down the drive, heading for the highway intersection.

With most of a tank of gas in her truck, she had no immediate need to stop. Speed counted now. Highway 277 would take her to 183, then to 283, and on into Altus.

She'd specifically chosen Oklahoma so that Blacke would have to cross a state line and violate his parole. Leaving Texas would land him right back in prison to serve those last six years of his sentence. Plus, Altus was a long way from Ward.

Two hours into the drive, she pulled over at the entrance to a pasture gate. Shifting into park, she scrolled through her calls to the hated number. With her heart in her throat, she called it.

A few rings later, the man she loathed was on the line. "Well, looky here who's calling me. Your boyfriend dead yet?"

His hateful voice was more than she could bear. "We have to talk. Altus, Oklahoma, the Regency Inn." She hung up and threw the phone in her bag, wiping her hand on her jeans to rid herself of his taint.

Let the bastard come after her now. She was through with running.

Adrenaline kept her awake on the last hours of the drive. Darkness hid the red-dirt Oklahoma land, but the Sooner State's flat horizon revealed the lights of small towns fifty miles before she came near them. Her heart ached for the pain Ward would feel when he woke to find her gone. She'd left him a note on the kitchen counter, telling him she had a plan and that when Blacke was no longer a threat, she'd return.

No matter how she looked at her situation, it was the only solution that kept Ward safe. And that was what mattered. He'd take a bullet for her in a heartbeat, and she couldn't let that happen. Blacke was too conniving to get caught before he killed someone. He wasn't going to stop. This was her problem, and it was up to her to solve it.

At not quite seven in the morning, using the GPS on her phone, she had no trouble finding the Regency Inn in Altus. It had cheap rates, and that was what mattered. She had money, but she wasn't rich. Blacke needed to find her fast.

Handing her debit card over to the clerk, she registered in the small, plain, hotel lobby. "A man from Texas will be here looking for me. I'd appreciate it if you'd send him on down to my room. Would you pass that on to the next shift please?"

The man gave her an odd look, but nodded.

She knew she was a mess—her face was all swollen and bruised and she had a big bandage on the side of her head. She grimaced. She didn't give a damn what the guy thought, as long as he did what she asked.

Her room was standard-issue chain-hotel accommodation—a double bed, nightstand, TV, dresser, and chair. She threw her bag on the bed. The first order of business was a shower. There was probably still blood in her hair. She wished she'd thought about snagging some bandages and tape at Ward's, but that had been the last thing on her mind.

She didn't linger. She had to stay on her guard. Wrapped in a towel, she stepped back into the bedroom. Her phone showed a missed call and a voice mail. It was Ward.

She sank down on the bed. Picking up the phone, tears welling in her eyes, she held it to her breast. He knew she was gone. The poor man, he'd be desperate, wondering if she were safe, where she was. She felt like a criminal.

She couldn't bear to listen to the voice mail. Not right then. Finding a pharmacy and a place to eat breakfast came first.

Google helped her find a nearby pharmacy, where she bought antibiotic ointment and bandages for her head. She applied them in the truck using the rearview mirror.

After that, it didn't take her long to come across a diner. As she walked inside, the overwhelming smell of bacon and coffee slammed into her, sending her tummy roiling. She ordered breakfast and made use of their bottomless-cup policy. Worrying about Ward kept her busy. The man must be out of his mind. Guilt swelled in her throat until it closed off. She threw down a tip and stood. If Blacke came calling, she wanted to be in her room.

After paying her bill, she strode out to the truck. As she slid inside, she grabbed her phone. It held two more missed calls and voice mails. *Oh, Ward. Honey, I'm so sorry. Please forgive me.* With shaking hands, she inserted the key into the ignition.

Ward's agonized face was before her as she drove. She bit her lip, doubting her plan. How could she hurt Ward this way? Had she been wrong to leave him? She sucked in air and gritted her teeth. No. She had to do this. It was the only way.

As she neared the hotel, she scanned the parking lot for Blacke's truck, but she didn't see it. Before going to her room, she stopped in at the office to see if anyone had been looking for her. No one had. Now the hard part began.

ONCE INSIDE THE ROOM, she put her gun on the nightstand. Sitting there on the bed, waiting, she tried to figure out what Ward had done when he'd found out she'd left. Was he furious with her? The knowledge that her leaving had hurt him was almost unbearable.

Drawing Blacke away like this was the only way she knew to protect Ward. She had to focus on that. She couldn't lose her resolve. She got up and paced the length of the room.

Striding back and forth from the chair to the bed, her stomach churned over what Ward must be going through. At last, she couldn't stand it any longer. Sitting on the bed, she listened to his first voice mail.

"Jayme, I woke up and you were gone. Where are you? You can't do this. You have to come back. It's too dangerous out there. Please, call me. Call me as soon as you get this. I need to know where you are. I love you."

He loved her? Her heart leapt and then thudded slowly in her chest. She lay back on the bed and drew her arm over her eyes. *Lord God, I can't bear it. He doesn't deserve to be hurt like this.* Tears rolled down into her hair. She lay still for a long time, trying to think of another way to keep Ward safe.

She played his second voice mail, unable to help herself, yet dreading hearing his painful words.

"Jayme, you haven't called. You can't leave like this. It's not safe. You know it. That bastard will kill you. Come back. We'll get through this. You've got to call me, sweetheart. Please, just call me. I love you."

The third was the worst of all.

"Jayme." His voice broke. *"Honey, I can't lose you. It can't happen again. Tell me where you are. I'll come. Please. Don't do this. I love you."*

She rolled over, clutching the phone to her chest. This strong, hard man had cried for her. It was too much. She sobbed into the pillow until her throat was raw.

When, at last, she ran out of tears, she got up and blew her nose. She couldn't let him suffer like this. She called him back.

He answered on the first ring, his voice hoarse and full of tension. "Jayme? Where are you? Tell me and I'll come. God, I've been worried sick, honey. I'm so glad you called."

Unlike the strong, independent man she knew, he was babbling. What had she done to him? "I just called to tell you I'm okay. I'm so sorry I worried you. I want to explain."

"Where are—"

"Ward, I left because I want you safe."

"Dammit, Jayme. Don't do this. We—"

The urgency, the anguish in his voice pierced her heart. "Just let me talk—please?"

He sighed loudly. "Okay."

"Blacke is my problem. I can't bear it that you got hurt. I won't let that happen again. I'm—"

"You can't—"

"Ward!"

He groaned.

"I need to handle this by myself. I have a plan. When I'm done, I'll come back, okay?"

"Jayme, this is crazy! You know Blacke better than anyone. You can't take him on. Please, please, honey, let me come help you."

Her chin trembled. "Ward, the whole point of me being here is to be far away from you. You're safe now. Listen. I want to tell you something... I love you, too."

"Aw, Jayme, honey, don't you see? You're—"

"I have to do this, Ward. Please, just let me do this. And try not to worry. I'll be careful."

Disconnecting, she lay back on the bed. Weak, almost ill, she let her phone ring and ring. A minute later, she had a new voice mail.

Please, God, protect me—and get Blacke here soon.

Chapter Seventeen

Jayme's cell went off. Ward again. God, she hated this. She couldn't stand ignoring him, knowing that it scared and hurt him.

She paced the room. Each time she faced the bed, she saw Dusty's photo on the nightstand. He was the main reason this had to end. She would never allow Blacke to get to him.

What if Blacke didn't come? What if she'd laid waste to Ward's heart for nothing? Everything depended on the depth of Blacke's hate—on his willingness to follow her.

She knew his wicked nature. The man who had raped and beaten her—the man who had hated her through nine long years in prison—this man had followed her across Texas for his revenge. He wouldn't stop now.

A raucous pounding sounded at the door.

Her heart froze.

Grabbing her phone and gun, she peered through the judas hole.

Her nightmare glared back at her.

Calling 911 with the phone on speaker, she strode to the bathroom and shut the door.

"911, what is your emergency?"

"I'm Jayme Bonner. Room 111 at the Regency Inn. Send the police."

The incredible pounding on the door continued. She prayed the bolts would hold.

"Dirk Blacke, a rapist and parole violator, is at my door. Hurry."

Leaving the call on speaker, she walked back into the bedroom and dropped her phone on the bed.

Standing by the chair, she yelled, "Blacke, leave me and mine alone. Nobody else needs to get hurt." She hoped he'd see reason. That she wouldn't need her gun.

Blacke shouted, "Open up, and we'll discuss it."

"I won't open the door. I know you're packing."

The door boomed thunderously and shook in its frame. Then it boomed again, and with a loud crack, the jamb splintered, the door exploding back against the wall.

Blacke barreled into the room and spotted her, her gun raised in defense.

He dove straight at her.

"No!" Him coming toward her was the last thing she'd expected. Fear slammed her, and time slowed, every detail crisp and clear.

Her aim went high and wide, and the slug struck him in the upper arm.

His body rammed into hers.

They both tumbled to the floor.

Her gun lay high on her chest, pinned between them.

He tried to wrangle it from her.

She pulled the trigger again.

The bullet tore upwards through his chin.

Time froze. She lay still. Her mind blanked. She didn't feel Blacke's dead weight. She didn't see the stains of him on the ceiling.

Sirens blared out front.

A policeman entered the shattered doorway, his gun drawn. He searched the rooms and called, "Clear!" Another came through the door. The first officer leaned into his shoulder mic. "Send an ambulance to the Regency Inn, Room 111."

He strode over to Jayme. "Ma'am, are you okay?" After gently maneuvering the gun from her hand, he gave it to the officer behind him. He checked Blacke's pulse, then rolled his lifeless body off her.

Suddenly free of Blacke's weight, she moaned. Time started again.

"Are you shot?"

"Uh, no. No, I'm not." She sat up slowly. "I've got... I have to... The bathroom." The gore on her face—she had to get it off.

The policeman helped her stand, and she rushed into the bathroom. *Oh God, oh God, oh God.*

He followed her. "Ma'am, I'm sorry, but you can't wash your hands. Procedure—we'll test your hands for residue."

"No! My face..." *No, no, no, no, no...*

"Hang on." He murmured to the other policeman, who disappeared out the door for a couple of minutes.

She stood, weaving back and forth, nausea cramping her stomach. *No, no, no, no, no...*

The officer reappeared and handed her a pair of disposable gloves. "Please leave the door open."

She snatched them and put them on. Avoiding looking in the mirror, she turned on the hot water. When steam rose from the sink, she wet a washcloth, covered it with soap, and scrubbed and scrubbed her face. She ran the cloth through her hair several times, trying to get the gooey mess out. *It's not working. It's not working!* She scrubbed harder, her hair flying in all directions.

The first policeman, who had waited patiently near the door, stepped closer and placed his hand over hers, stilling it. "We need to talk, ma'am."

She sobbed, "It's still there."

He stepped beside her and examined her head. "I think you got it, ma'am. You're okay now."

Closing her eyes, she clutched the edge of the sink. Her stomach heaved, and she threw the washcloth on the floor, covering her mouth. She took a quick breath. "Okay, just a minute." Grabbing a T-shirt out of the bag on her bed, she locked herself inside the bathroom and ripped off her soiled shirt. She threw it in the trash, along with the gloves. After dragging the new one over her head, she stepped out the door.

The EMTs had arrived, and another policeman had shown up, too. Blacke's body lay stretched across the floor. The smell of gunpowder and violent death weighed heavily in the air. A thick wave of nausea hit her like a punch in the gut. She swallowed hard as she felt the blood drain from her face. *God, don't let me faint.*

Turning to the policeman, she asked, "Can we go outside?"

Unsteady on her feet, she leaned up against the outer wall and told him what had gone down in the room. It amazed her that she could speak so calmly about it. She'd just killed a man.

The policeman stepped inside for a few seconds and came back out. "Let's go down to the station. You'll be a lot more comfortable there. And you can start from the beginning."

"Can you get my purse and my phone? And I need to make a quick call."

WARD LEANED INTO THE center console of Casey's truck. Even with the seat cranked all the way back, his cast leg still barely fit. It ached like hell, a fact that didn't make thinking about this mess any easier.

Casey glanced over. "How you doing?"

"I'm shitty, thank you."

He slapped his hand on the dash and it sounded like a pistol shot. "What the hell was her plan? She said she was protecting me. Doesn't she realize it would kill me if something happened to her?" His hand shook, and he made a fist. He had to get a hold of himself.

Clenching his teeth, he stared out the window. Was loving Jayme the biggest mistake of his life? He'd barely survived losing his wife and son. This woman was a risk taker. Big time.

Casey ignored the speed limit, careening through the curves and going all out on the straightaways.

Nothing eased Ward's anxiety. Jayme needed him. Would she be charged with murder? How long would they keep her in Altus?

She must have called Blacke. How could she have imagined that this situation would turn out well? She was crazy to have taken a chance like this. His chest tightened as his anxiety ratcheted even higher. "Dammit, can't this thing go any faster?"

They had a little more than three hours to go before they hit Altus.

AS SOON AS THEY PULLED up to the police station, Ward threw open his door. There'd be hell to pay if they'd thrown Jayme in a cell. This man had come after her, by God. He gritted his teeth as he grabbed his leg and levered it out of the truck. *Dammit! Of all the times for me to be hobbling around on crutches.*

Once inside the building, he knocked on the clear walls of the administrative cubicle.

A woman in uniform came out from its adjacent room. "Hi, can I help you?"

"My name's Ward Ramsey. I'm looking for Jayme Bonner. She was brought here after an incident at the Regency Inn. I'm a friend of hers. Can someone tell me what's going on?"

The woman said. "Detective Thompson is with her now."

"Would you do me a favor? Can you tell Detective Thompson I'm here? I can corroborate her story. And, please, can you let Jayme know, too?"

"Let me go take a look. Find out what's going on. Have a seat, why don't you?"

Ward blew out a short breath and glanced at the clock on the far wall, unable to tolerate the idea of sitting down. But he did move away from the window.

Casey squeezed his shoulder. "I hope to hell they're not making trouble for her in there. She's been through enough."

Ward clenched his hands into fists. "I just don't get what she was doing. What did she think would happen when she set this up?"

Casey looked at him and sighed. "Honestly? I think she was through with living in fear. She figured something exactly like this was going to happen. At least, she hoped it would turn out like this."

Ward looked at the floor, fear making his voice shake. "It could have been her in a body bag."

About twenty minutes later, Detective Thompson came out. "Ward Ramsey?"

Relief flooded him, and he struggled to his feet as the detective walked over. "Yes?"

"Jim Thompson." He offered his hand. "Miss Bonner's not under arrest. I talked to Sheriff Bryant down in Haskell County, and he filled me in. The officers on the scene have spoken with me. And we have the 911 recording of the man breaking into her room."

Pointing to Ward's leg, he said, "I see the evidence here of the wreck Miss Bonner told me about. Things look pretty straightforward. I just checked in over at the crime scene, and they're done. She can go back to the hotel and pick up her stuff when she leaves here. The officers had the staff pack it up and take it to the office since the door was busted in. We'll be keeping the shirt she was wearing, though. I just need to hang onto her for a little while longer for some paperwork, and then she can go. I know where to reach her if we need anything as we move forward with the investigation."

Another long hour dragged by before Detective Thompson walked back out, followed by a visibly tired and shaken Jayme.

Ward pulled her into a hug. She melted into his arms, boneless and frail-seeming. "Thank God you're okay." Then he couldn't talk anymore. He could only hang on with all his strength.

Pulling back with a frown, she said, "I was worried you were trying to drive." She turned to Casey. "Thanks so much for bringing him here. Though I'm sure he didn't give you much choice."

He grinned. "What are friends for?"

She gave Ward a wan smile. "Thank you for coming." She kissed him quickly and stood back. "Detective Thompson said I can pick up my stuff."

"Come on. Let's go." Ward followed her out the door Casey held open for them. After the agony of the drive to Altus, his relief at having her with him nearly overwhelmed him. It was starting to soak in that she was safe. But, God, she looked terrible. Her shoulders slumped, and she seemed barely able to put one foot in front of the other. He needed to hold her in his arms, to reassure her that she was safe, that she'd be okay, despite what had happened.

A few minutes later, they pulled up to the hotel and parked in front. Jayme got her bag and threw it in the cab of her truck. She came back over and leaned on Ward's window.

Her slack expression told him everything he needed to know about her frame of mind. He cupped her face in his hand. "Do you feel like getting something to eat, honey? You should try to eat."

Raising her eyes, she nodded.

He could tell she didn't feel up to much but she probably hadn't eaten all day. She needed to get something in her belly. "We'll just try, okay?"

They took both trucks and drove until they found a steakhouse. Once inside, he put his arm around her as they waited to be seated. She seemed so fragile. How come he'd never noticed that before? She held her arms folded across her chest, as if for protection, and it nearly did him in.

She shrugged away from him. "I'm going to the ladies' room. I'll catch you at the table."

The two men had been seated for more than ten minutes when Jayme found them.

She sat next to Ward and picked up her menu, her eyes puffy and red.

He reached under the table and patted her leg, squeezing it gently. He hurt when she hurt. That's what came with loving her. Healing would take time, but surely there was something he could do now, tonight, to help her.

The waitress came over. "You all ready to order?"

He looked at Jayme. "You probably need more time, don't you?"

Closing her menu, she said, "I think I'll just have a chef's salad and iced tea."

He wanted to protest but thought better of it. "I'll have a T-bone and a baked potato."

Casey handed his menu to the waitress. "Same here."

Ward tried not to stare at Jayme. He sensed her deeply troubled mood and couldn't imagine how she felt after killing Blacke. The sorry bastard. Killing him would scar Jayme for the rest of her life. In a way, the bastard had gotten his revenge, and that just made Ward sick.

They ate a quiet dinner. No one knew what to say, and Jayme didn't seem to want to talk.

He paid the check, and they walked outside, slowing to accommodate his pace.

He touched Casey's arm. "Let's find a different hotel. I'm paying, of course. It's way too late to start back now."

"Will that leg of yours fit in Jayme's truck?"

He turned to her. "Your seat slide back?"

She nodded.

"Should do."

"Then I'd just as soon drive back home tonight. I don't mind night driving, and I have a lot going on tomorrow."

Ward put out his hand. "Sure thing, partner. Don't know how I can thank you."

Casey gave him a hug instead. "Don't have to. Just come visit more often." He kissed Jayme's cheek and hugged her. "You listen here. I'm counting on you to keep this guy in line while he's all banged up. No more running off."

Jayme smiled. "I promise." Her smile didn't last long.

Wishing he could put his arm around her as they headed to her truck, Ward silently cursed his damn crutches. He settled for, "I got you, honey. Don't you worry about a thing."

They drove until he pointed out a Quality Inn a few blocks ahead. "Let's stop there, see if they have a room."

When Jayme parked in front of the hotel, he reached out and touched her arm. "Would you stay in a room with me tonight?" The haunted look in her eyes nearly broke his heart.

If she didn't agree, he'd just have to convince her. No way was he letting her sleep alone tonight. Not after she'd killed a man.

She bit her bottom lip for a moment, then nodded.

"Great." He gave her his credit card and waited for her to pay for a room for them. He'd seen her eyes—her face—change in the silence while she ate. No matter what it took, he'd do his best to drive those thoughts away.

Jayme came back out, and they drove around to a ground floor room on the back side of the hotel.

Jayme stood watching him drag his leg out of the truck, her face solemn.

Grinning, he said, "Not so hard."

Handing him his crutches, she said, "You're getting pretty good at that."

"I'll be running before you know it."

She patted his back but had no smile for him.

He frowned at her worn, drawn face. They had to get to the room and settle in so he could hold her in his arms. Somehow, he had to take this burden from her. She was shutting down.

As soon as they walked in the door, Jayme headed to the bathroom. "I'm taking a shower." She disappeared inside with her bag.

His eyes followed her until the door shut. He had something to say tonight. Something that could make all the difference in the world.

Chapter Eighteen

W ard glanced around the room. Just the basics—no minibar. Too bad. He wished he had a stiff drink to give Jayme. Anything to break the pall that had fallen over her.

The stale air told him the room hadn't been used in a while. Hobbling over to the air-conditioning unit under the window, he kicked it down several notches until he was sure it would cool the room off. After hanging his shirt in the closet and taking off his shoes, he made his way to the bed.

Propping a couple of pillows behind him, he turned on the TV, letting his mind drift to the mindless noise. Jayme was safe. Now he could breathe again. Life could return to normal.

Except it couldn't. Jayme was a mess. Anybody could see it. How the hell did he comfort her? He didn't know what to say. It should have been him that killed the bastard. He'd give anything to change what happened today. Now he had to find a way to get through to her. Help her begin to heal.

She stayed in the shower for a full hour. When she came out, she looked pink and worn in a tank top and shorts. She set her bag by the table and climbed up on the bed.

"Come here, baby." He pulled her down on his chest. She snuggled in, and he kissed the top of her head. "I was beginning to think you'd drowned in there."

"Nope. Just getting clean." Her voice was slightly above a whisper.

He sniffed her hair. "You always smell so good. I never told you that I love the way you smell."

Smiling into his chest, she said, "Thanks. I like the way you smell, too."

"Really?"

"Uh-hm. I call it leather and oak. Makes me feel safe."

"Well, hell. I'll have to remember that for all my other girl-friends."

She pinched his stomach, and he felt her lips move in a smile again.

"Ow! Okay, I'll save it for you, then." She seemed a little better. The shower had done her some good. God, she was gorgeous. Even now, with everything she'd been through, her beauty drew his body like a bee to honey.

"I forgot about something, anyway."

Sighing, she kept her eyes closed. "What?" she asked softly.

"I only have one very special girlfriend."

She lifted her head and stared at him. "Just one?"

He'd waited too long to do this. Reaching down, he un-zipped a pocket in his cargo shorts. Fumbling around inside, he pulled out a small box and opened it.

"Yep, just one." He held up the ring, grinning at her aston-ished face. "Jayme Bonner, I love you. I want you with me for all my days and all my nights—for the rest of my life. Will you marry me?"

She jerked upright. She looked at the ring, then looked at him, then looked at the ring again.

He sat up, too, worried now at what she might say.

Throwing her arms around his neck, she said fiercely. "Yes, I'll marry you. All of my days and all of my nights, I'll love you and be by your side."

He held her, and she was quiet. This moment—having her—made the worry, the fear, the danger...everything, worth it.

She sniffed. Then did it again.

"Honey, you okay?" He wanted to look into her eyes, but she kept them averted. Tilting her chin up, he got what he needed.

Wiping her eyes, she said, "Today doesn't deserve... This was the second most horrible day of my life." She bit her lip. "And now... Ward, this is the most beautiful thing that's ever happened to me. And it—" She sucked in a ragged breath, a quiet sob escaping her lips.

Still holding the ring, he wrapped her in his arms and lay back down on the pillows. "Hush, honey. It's okay." Lord, he had to help her—had to find the right words. Was giving her the ring tonight a mistake?

After a few seconds, she took a deep breath and pulled away. "No, wait, Ward. I want to finish. This beautiful gift you've given me came on a day I killed a man. A man I hated. And someday, I'll have to explain to my son that I killed his father."

His eyes widened, and he nodded slowly. Everything made more sense now. Her running, Dusty, their life. Easing her back down into his arms, he snuggled her head under his chin. "Jayme. I'm so sorry. I never knew that last bit. It's an awful thing." He brushed her hair back from her face and cupped her cheek. "But I'll be there with you when you tell Dusty. We'll do it together."

Lacing his fingers through hers, he said, "Let me tell you why I gave you this tonight." Then he slipped the ring a little way down her finger. "When you left without telling me, and that bastard was out there hunting you, the only thing I could think was, 'I never told her how much I loved her. I never asked her to marry me.'"

He squeezed her tight. God, how good loving her felt. "Remember when you slept in the guest bedroom, and Casey came and stayed with you? I bought this ring when I went into town. Casey knew something was fishy. I told him when we shared your story about Blacke that day that I was asking you to marry me. I wanted to take you out to dinner and make some kind of wonderful, romantic proposal like you deserve."

Cupping her head in his hand again, he kissed her forehead, then tilted her head so he could look into her eyes. "But all this made me realize that you never know what the next day will bring. I promised myself that, as soon as we were alone, I'd ask you to marry me."

"You're right. We don't know what's ahead of us." Then she slid the ring all the way down her finger and showed him her hand.

He pulled her fingers to his lips and kissed them. "The future Mrs. Ramsey. I sure never thought I'd say that." Having her as his wife was the culmination to his fantasy of loving her. What he found hard to believe was that this proud, independent woman had chosen to love him, even after he'd treated her so badly. She must have X-ray vision to have seen beyond the asshole to the good guy inside.

With a smile that overcame the sadness in her face, at least for a while, she tucked into him, wrapping her leg around his good one.

In a little while, he sighed. "I'd give my right arm to take a shower. This damned cast. I haven't been able to clean up good since before the accident."

Jayme sat up and gave a crisp nod. "I might have the answer to that." She lifted up the trash bag out of the can by the table, looking for the stash of clean bags she knew the maid would probably have left in the bottom. She grabbed them and sat down again. "I'll tie these on you, and you can take a shower. Just a quick one."

The hot water felt amazing on the stiff muscles of his back. How long had it been since things had been normal? As he scrubbed shampoo into his hair with one hand while his other clutched the safety bar, his mind wandered to Jayme and the fact that they'd be sharing a bed tonight. Not that he'd let anything happen. But snuggling with her? Oh, yeah. He had to concentrate to calm himself down. His arousal was the last thing the poor woman needed to see when he walked out. There'd be plenty of time for that. Ten minutes later, he came out of the bathroom wrapped in a towel and hobbling on his crutches.

"How about taking this wet plastic off me?"

Jayme unwrapped his cast. It had stayed relatively dry. This would be a working solution.

After helping him into bed, she climbed in herself. She'd lost the deadness in her face while he was gone.

Settling her gently on his chest, he stroked her back, brushing her hair away from her cheek as he kissed her tenderly.

"You'll be okay. I want you to talk to me whenever what happened today messes with you. And it will. It's going to take time for you to get back to being yourself." He'd be watching for signs that she wasn't doing well. If she didn't bring it up, he would.

Nodding into his chest, she said, "I'll try."

The intensity of his feelings astounded him. He could barely remember his cold, hard life before she walked into his barn. Every day now, he woke up wanting to get the morning started. Wanting to see her face first thing. The chance that she'd turned up at his ranch, in the whole, wide state of Texas, was one in a million.

Jayme sighed and settled her head into his shoulder, draping her arm across his chest and tucking her leg around his. He marveled at the way she fit him perfectly. Stroking her sweet-smelling hair, he kissed her forehead. For the first time in ten years, everything was right in his world.

JAYME PUT HER HANDS on her hips. "Dusty, we can't go fishing until you finish up your chores." Her boy had been ecstatic since he saw her ring and found out that she and "Mr. Ramsey" were getting married. He could hardly talk about anything else.

She got the broom out of the closet and started sweeping the living room. Things had been hectic since that terrible day in Oklahoma. She and Annie had worked hard on wedding plans. The event had turned into much more than Jayme had bargained for. She'd figured on a small wedding, inviting just her dad, Casey and Annie, and maybe a few more people.

Annie had nixed that in a heartbeat. Her take was that Ward Ramsay remarrying was an epic day in the history of Haskell County, and that all his friends—and there were many—needed to be there to witness it. Ward had agreed with Annie, saying that people would be hurt if they weren't invited.

She couldn't understand how it worked, but every day her love for Ward grew. She didn't know a heart could hold so much love. She'd thought her heart was full to the brim with love for Dusty, but it had turned out that there was oodles of room for this man too.

The doctor who'd taken over Ward's care here in Haskell had assured him that his cast would come off before the ceremony.

She and Ward were headed to Cabo San Lucas, Mexico, for their honeymoon. Dusty would stay with Casey and Annie, and Ward had asked Cash to feed the stock while they were gone.

Scooting her pile of dirt into the dustpan, she dumped it in the trash. As if planning a wedding wasn't enough, she did most of the work around the ranch too. It was weird. Working during the day without Ward made her miss him so much that she rushed through every chore, hoping to get home just a little bit sooner.

She and Dusty had moved into the spare bedroom at the ranch house. Not only because she loved Ward, but because everything he did was so much harder on crutches. She took care of as much as the stubborn man would let her.

Ward swung into the living room on his "sticks," as he called them, having been out in the far pasture on the Kawasaki Mule. The small four-wheel-drive vehicle was his saving grace.

What she would have done if he didn't have that freedom, she couldn't imagine. She gave him a peck on the cheek as joy swept through her. She'd missed him.

Dusty grinned like crazy. Her boy was happy as a hog in a mud pit whenever he saw them kiss.

"Those chores finished yet?"

"Almost, Momma."

Ward shook his head. "I can hear those big old fish jumping from here. You'd better hurry."

She'd packed a picnic supper earlier for them to eat at the pond and was looking forward to sitting on the tailgate while the boys fished.

Ward was on the couch, so she sat down and snuggled into his arms. Would she ever get used to how wonderful this felt? She rested her head against his chest, breathing him in.

He picked up her hand and examined it in the light. "Soon you'll have another ring to go with this one."

She shivered unexpectedly. Her heart had never known the kind of love she felt for this handsome, extraordinary man. "I can't wait." She kissed him, slowly, making it last since Dusty wasn't in the room. Two more days to go.

Grinning, he said, "Tomorrow I get this damned ball and chain off my leg."

Smiling impishly, she said, "Just in time for the fun and gam—"

"I'm done with my chores, Mom."

Ward laughed. "Yep. Just in time."

THE LATE EVENING SUN warmed Jayme's face as she swung her feet back and forth on the tailgate. The cool breeze coming off the pond tickled her with the strands of hair that had escaped her ponytail. Her world was so different now. So full of love and happiness. How had she been content before? Ward had shown her that men could be kind and trustworthy. She'd never realized how burdened she was by fear and distrust until that weight had lifted from her shoulders. She and Ward would be a team, loving and supporting each other, through good times and bad.

Dusty caught a crappie, and Ward watched him haul back and cast again. Ward's intensity and focus touched her, as always. When he and Dusty were fishing, everyone else might as well not exist.

Ward went over and slung his arm around Dusty's shoulders, saying something she couldn't hear. Dusty raised his face to Ward and grinned as he reeled his line in. Those two adored each other. She clasped her hands together, her heart overflowing. Her boy finally had a daddy. And, soon, she'd have a husband. Imagine that.

Chapter Nineteen

Τhe plane dropped swiftly toward the runway. Jayme clenched the armrests. She'd never flown before and, much as she understood that flying was safe, it sure didn't seem that way when the ground was speeding toward her faster than a runaway horse. The tires bumped the tarmac, and the overwhelming sound of the engines cycling down tore at her ears. Squeezing harder, she pressed her head into the seat back. *Lord, let me survive this. I've come too far to die now.*

Ward patted her hand and half shouted over the noise. "We're safe, honey. Now the fun starts."

She tried to smile but didn't quite make it. With her eyes squeezed shut, she settled for a nod.

THE EVENING WAS GONE by the time they made it through customs and found a taxi to take them to the hotel. Cabo San Lucas didn't disappoint her. Beautiful palm trees and flowering foliage she couldn't name were everywhere. She rolled the taxi's window down for the rich scent of the warm ocean breeze, then reached for Ward's hand, wanting the intimacy of his touch, anticipating other intimacies the night would bring. He leaned over and nibbled her ear, and she sucked in a breath as tingling goose bumps pebbled her arms.

This man made her body dance with the slightest trace of his fingertips, and she couldn't wait to have him all to herself.

When they arrived, Ward wanted to carry both suitcases, but she insisted on carrying her own. In her book, he was still one of the walking wounded.

Their hotel was on the beach, and the room faced the rolling waves a short walk away. Ward had hired a travel planner, and she'd handled everything for them. They had snorkeling lessons booked, jet skis rented, and, of course, they'd shop in the picturesque town. She glanced at her husband as they walked toward their room. In profile he resembled the Ramsey she'd met on her first day on the ranch, but nothing else remained to remind her of that cold, hard man. This Ward was warm and loving, intimate and sharing. She loved every square inch of him and couldn't wait to start life as his wife.

The low roar of the incoming tide caught her attention. Moonlight settled atop the incoming breakers. This was a perfect ending to the perfect day. Her morning wedding had been flawless. Annie had been her matron of honor and Casey Ward's best man. Dusty, of course, had been the ring bearer. Jayme had met so many of Ward's good friends. After all her years of traveling, she could finally say she had a home. The best part of all had been the intense, loving look in Ward's eyes when he'd slipped the wedding band on her finger. At that moment, she'd felt her old life, her lonely past, fall away.

Ward unlocked their door, and they stepped inside. He dropped his bag and shut the door to the lovely, cabana-style room. "Come here."

His command sent a shiver of pleasure up her spine. The quiet timbre of his voice had cast a spell. She could barely breathe.

He reached out his hand, molding his white dress shirt to his powerful shoulder. His brown eyes seemed black in the soft light.

When she slid her hand into his, he tugged her closer and, without breaking eye contact, slipped his fingers under the hem of her white sheath.

Shivers shot up her belly. She placed her hand on his chest, feeling the hard muscle beneath his shirt.

Slowly, inch by inch, his hand caressed her thigh, finally coming to rest on the curve of her butt.

She sighed and closed her eyes, tilting her head back.

He leaned in and kissed her in the spot behind her ear that drove her wild. A high-pitched moan escaped her mouth.

Nibbling on her neck, he said, "I sure do love the way you look in this dress, Mrs. Ramsey. Maybe you should buy more of these."

Her lips pouted. "And just where would I wear them, Mr. Ramsey?" She loved him in this mood.

"You let me worry about that."

He gave her a lingering kiss and pulled back. "You think there's still room service?"

Excitement from his touch still rippling through her, she stepped back and looked for the phone. "I'll find out." She called and found that room service ran until midnight. "Grab the menu. We have twelve minutes."

They made their choices and, while Ward called in the order, she announced, "First dibs on the shower. I won't be long."

One of the things Annie had helped her do was shop for lingerie. It had turned out that ladies' underthings were a whole new world, and Annie sure knew how to navigate it. Now Jayme wondered if she had the nerve to wear the stuff.

She showered quickly. Dinner was delivered as she slid on her babydoll negligee—a short, black, lacy thing that exposed more of her breasts than anything she'd ever worn. Wondering if she looked ridiculous, she gathered her courage and stepped out of the bathroom.

Ward was bent over the table, laying out their food. He turned when the door opened and froze, then dropped what he had in his hands and was instantly beside her. With a huge smile on his face, he said, "Jayme, baby, you look—just beautiful."

"You like it? I didn't know. It's a little—"

"What? Honey, I like it. I love it. Are you kidding?"

He pulled her into his arms.

She slid her arms around his neck and kissed him slowly, teasing him. Tonight, she'd show this man just how much she loved him.

He tugged her toward the table. "Let's eat." He gave her a crazy grin. "You're going to need your strength."

Later, Ward walked out of the bathroom in a pair of blue athletic shorts. "They don't make fancy duds for men on their wedding night."

She grinned and wiggled her eyebrows. "You don't need no fancy duds, boy. Get over here." There wasn't a man alive who was more gorgeous than her new husband. She smiled and pulled back the covers to let him into bed.

As he slid in beside her, his familiar leather-and-oak scent enveloped her.

Closing her eyes, she breathed in and out. "You smell good."

He leaned in and kissed her, nibbling her earlobe and her throat.

Shivers skittered along her spine. She ran her hand up his arm, resting it on his shoulder. He was so strong, so protective of her. Her very own guardian angel. It was a luxury she was still getting used to.

"You smell good too. You always do. Even when we're working. How do you do that?"

She gave an unladylike snort. "It's your overactive imagination."

Laughing, he said, "No way. You do. I noticed clear back when you first started working for me. It drove me nuts."

"Really?" The only thing she remembered about that time was what a bastard he had been.

"Yeah. Why do you think I was such a grouch?"

"I just thought you were an asshole."

He cracked up and tucked her hair behind her ear, tracing the line of her jaw with his fingers and dropping a kiss on the tip of her nose. "Well, I was an asshole. But you and your wonderful smell weren't helping things. Everything about you attracted me, and I didn't want that."

"Well, you sure as hell knew how to hide it." She tried to imagine the Ward she remembered, the asshole, the jerk, the man who never spoke her name, being attracted to her, and she had to giggle.

"Ah, Jayme. I'm so glad you stuck around. You took every-thing I threw at you and came back for more. That's when you started getting to me."

"I quit thinking you were a bastard about the time you started hugging on my boy."

"Dusty's one in a million."

Ward looked into her eyes and smiled while his fingers toyed with the hem of her gown. "I like this. It shows off some of my favorite things about you." He grinned wickedly.

She narrowed her eyes. "Really."

"Uh-huh." Leaning in, he nibbled on her neck, flicking her with his tongue and placing tiny kisses all the way to her aching breasts.

Her breath caught, and a fire started in her belly. She pressed up into his mouth. Grazing his cheek with her finger-tips, she pulled him up, the tender look in his eyes everything that she longed for.

He covered her mouth with his, slanting his lips across hers and angling his head for deeper access as he probed with his tongue. He tasted minty and earthy. She wanted more. She twined her tongue with his, learning him. Heat radiated from his body and seeped into her skin. With their mouths as one, he pressed his erection against her belly, thrusting with the same rhythm of his tongue in her mouth. She pushed her hips forward, straining to increase the contact of his hard body to her core. God, he made her want him.

Sliding his hand inside her gown, he cupped her breast, brushing his thumb across her sensitive nipple. "I think we need to take something off, don't you?"

Electrified with his touch, an intense burst of love washed through her.

He slid his hand to her hip and whispered in her ear, "Let's get rid of these."

She lifted her hips, and he pulled her panties down. They landed on the carpet. He lowered his mouth to hers, kissing her possessively, seeking her depths with his tongue.

Her blood raced with anticipation, and she grasped his lower lip with her teeth, sucking gently as a throaty moan escaped him. She wanted him hot. Wanted him needy. Wanted him to love her all night long.

Tracing his fingers across the lace on her negligee, he said, "Damn, I mean... How beautiful are you?"

"I guess this is the new me."

"Oh, hell yeah."

He leaned in and nibbled on her sensitive nipples through the fabric until they rose into taut pearls, sending delicious shivers through her.

"Ward, please." She was shocked at the way her words sounded like a pathetic plea.

"Please what?" His bold, seductive smile left no doubt as to who was in charge.

"You know damn well what, mister. If you don't put your mouth on me, I'll die."

"Anything you want, sweetheart. But first I think we need to take this off too." He lifted her negligee and drew it over her head. Closing his eyes, he held it to his face and inhaled, then slid it across his cheek. "Mm, nice." He dropped it on the floor.

The cold air from the air-conditioning vent blew over her nipples, puckering them harder, sending shivers down her belly.

In contrast, she could feel the heat as his hungry gaze roved over her. Her body responded to the look of love and desire in his eyes. The raw power of being wanted rushed through her.

He gave her his lopsided smile and uttered a thoroughly male growl as he quickly rid himself of his shorts. She smiled appreciatively and reached for him. Cupping her breasts, he squeezed lightly, massaging them until she wanted to cry from the sheer pleasure of his touch. He knew what she wanted, how she wanted it. It was as though he was made for her—her perfect man.

He slid his hand under her back and pulled her closer. Bending his head, he sucked her bare nipple into his mouth, caressing it with his tongue, rolling her other nipple between his thumb and forefinger. Shivery sensations cascaded through her.

She held his head, running her fingers through his dark hair. When he caught her nipple firmly between his teeth, she cried out. Moaning, she said, "How do you know?"

He kissed his way down her body, drawing tiny circles with his tongue around her navel. "Know what?"

The feather-light touch of his adoring fingertips intensified her tingling response. Her core was on fire, yearning for his caress. She could feel the heat of him against her skin. "Know what I need. What I want."

His warm hand spread her. His fingers slid between her folds. His lips tickled their way up her torso, and she sighed as he lowered his lips to her breast, circling her nipple with his tongue. He took it in his mouth and she arched into the suction, gasping at the twin seductions of his lips and fingers. She couldn't think. There was only him, his lips, his fingers, his touch.

Exhaling a breathless laugh, he said, "I know because I want it too. I'm going to kiss every inch of your gorgeous body tonight."

She stroked his hair, the warmth of his breath delicious on her bare skin, and stared up at the rough-hewn beam in the ceiling. Her long years of isolation were over. Her life would be full of this man's love, his safety and protection. God had filled her every need.

Ward trailed kisses down the roundness of her breast, on her tummy, and lower, stopping at her soft curls.

She was lost in a world of sensation. Every place he touched was exquisitely sensitive. Lifting her head, she said, "Take me now. Please, take me."

"Not yet, my love."

He slipped two fingers inside her slippery folds, pumping them in and out of her while at the same time rocking his hips against her. Lowering his lips to hers, he kissed her, softly at first, then harder as he pistoned his fingers faster. He whispered, "I love you, Jayme."

A powerful force built inside her. She gripped his shoulders and returned his urgent kiss.

Flicking his thumb over her sensitive bud, he stroked up and down, back and forth, around and around in ever tightening circles. He opened his mouth, breathing her panting breaths as she came closer and closer to the edge.

She rocked her hips, clutching him, wanting him. She whispered urgently, "Ward, Ward, now."

Grasping her hips, he trailed his lips down her torso and kissed her between the thighs, his tongue stroking up her soft folds. Her abdominal muscles bunched, and she cried out.

Breath quickening, she ground her head into the pillow, aching with need. Her fingers caressed his hair, and she moaned as he worked his magic, desire seeping through her pores, twining into colors that misted before her eyes.

She shattered. A maelstrom of light and color swirled in her mind. She pulled him to her, then turned over and rose up to her hands and knees with a need so urgent she couldn't speak.

Ward panted, "Oh, baby."

"Hurry," she gasped.

He drew her to him, easing into her slick warmth. "Ah, Jayme. My love." Drawing back, he pushed in again.

Trembling, needing him inside her, she said, "Now. Harder."

He pulled back and entered with a powerful thrust.

"Yes," she panted. Contractions shuddered through her body as he plunged into her again and again, rocking into her with his steady rhythm, branding her from the inside out. She tilted her hips, giving him full access to her depths. Tears of joy streamed down her face as Ward, his breath ragged, thrust one last time, pulsing deep inside her.

She collapsed on her belly as small contractions brought her pleasure.

Still inside her, he drew her into a spooning embrace.

She'd never been high, but this must be what it felt like, everything perfect, time nonexistent. She could stay this way, held in his loving arms, forever, and be happy.

Ward nuzzled her neck, kissing her tenderly. "I love you."

Each word fell as a blessing in her heart. She'd waited a lifetime for a man to say he loved her. She had no doubt she'd hear those words hundreds, maybe thousands of times from her husband. Tonight, she made a silent promise—she'd never grow complacent. She'd cherish Ward each time he said them. She clasped his hand and traced his wedding band with her fingertip. "I love you too."

Sneak Peek of Her Ride or Die Cowboy

Now that was some nice cowboy booty. Dallas Royle was usually too busy to notice the patrons of the Last Cowboy Standing dancehall unless they were lined up in front of her ordering drinks, but the handsome man walking by was a treat for her eyes as she leaned on the bar in an unusual lull.

Ignoring the pounding beat of the crazy-loud Red Dirt country coming from the stage, she watched him return to the small table he shared with two other cowboys. He chose a chair pointing in her direction. His face was as sexy as his backside, with a strong, square jaw, and high cheekbones. He was a handsome devil, that was for sure.

She rubbed the back of her neck and grabbed a wet towel, sweeping it across the slab of polished mesquite that made up the bar top. Her three-year-old daughter needed her mother focused on the right priorities, and a man was definitely not one of them. Piper had run a fever all day, coughing along with swiping at a runny nose. Pulling her phone out of her back pocket, she checked the time. Forty-five minutes until her break.

Dallas glanced at the dance floor, its polished wood a perfect surface for the fast-paced boot scootin' that went along with the rowdy songs the band usually played. A slow tune wafted through the air now, though. Cowboys held their girls close, swaying in a gentle two-step. Remembering what that felt like, she quickly shifted her gaze, then knelt to straighten some napkins and boxes under the bar. What was wrong with her tonight? Had she thrown her brain in the blender when she made that last frozen margarita? She had a plan for her life, and she was sticking to it.

The rare respite ended, and three people at once appeared at the bar. Straining to hear their orders over the new, much louder song, Dallas flitted from one to the other, efficiently handing out beers, mixing drinks, and making change. Other customers replaced them until she found herself face-to-face with the handsome cowboy.

He smiled and handed her a five-dollar bill, almost shouting, "Bud Light, please, ma'am. Keep the change."

Dallas pulled his longneck out of the ice, popped the top off, and returned to his place at the bar. As she returned his smile, she took in more details of his appearance. Amber eyes sparked with self-confidence. A sturdy, working-man's hand received the bottle she offered. His strong arms and broad shoulders stretched the material of his shirt. No doubt he could manhandle a 300-pound calf to the ground.

Raising the beer in salute, he said, "Thank you, ma'am," and turned away.

She had no time to watch him and his fine rear end walk away. Customers vied for her attention non-stop until a familiar face showed up. This cowboy had his arm slung over the shoulder of a young woman. Dallas frowned in surprise. Nearly every week the man came up to her bar with someone new, but last time he'd arrived with a girl wearing his engagement ring. How proud she'd been, even showing Dallas, saying the guy had just given her the sparkling solitaire. Now the jerk was standing here with a different woman. Gut-sick, Dallas scowled at the asshole as the loud pounding music beat at her senses. She spun away, shoving her hair behind her ear. *Let him wait for his beer.* Moving down to the other end of the bar, she waited on the next customer. Men were such bastards. The words *loyal* and *man* should never go in the same sentence.

A few minutes later, still ready to spit nails, Dallas nodded to the waitress who came to cover the bar for her break. Grabbing her phone and car keys, Dallas strode out of the saloon-style front doors into the parking lot. As always, her car sat in the back, so she turned the corner into the deepening darkness on the side of the building. She hurried past the trucks parked on her right, focused on her car ahead at the end.

A step from her car door she heard gravel crunching behind her. She grabbed for the door handle as a tall, heavyset cowboy clutched her arm. Yanking back, she tried to free herself, but he gripped her tightly.

"Hey there, pretty thing."

His slurred, drunken voice sent chills through her. Far from the front lot where others might hear her yell, she had no hope of help.

"Let go of me!" She jerked hard on her arm again. "Leave me alone, you creep!" She aimed a kick at his groin.

Suddenly the drunk's head smashed sideways into the top of her car. The good-looking cowboy's punch had landed perfectly, and he shoved the other man to the ground. "Go sleep it off in your truck before I call the police."

The drunk got up. He staggered to a Ford dually pick-up parked a few vehicles down the lot and got in.

Dallas rubbed her arm where the man had held her and stared at the cowboy. "Were you following me?" Still angry at the unfaithful cretin at the bar, she didn't come off as thankful as she should be.

"Nope. I'm parked over there, too. I was out here getting some fresh air when that bozo grabbed you. Figured you needed help."

"Oh." What a relief. He didn't seem like a stalker, either. "Well, thanks. Wish employees didn't have to park all the way back here." Reluctantly, she reached out her hand. "My name's Dallas, by the way."

"Cash Powers. Pleased to meet you." His clasp was gentle.

"I need to call my mom. That's why I came out here. My daughter's been sick, and I'm worried about her. So..." She glanced at her car door and back. "Thanks again."

Tipping his hat, he backed up a step, turned around, and walked toward the front of the building.

Dallas narrowed her eyes. He was so darn good to look at, but that didn't matter. Experience had proved that her decision to keep men at a long arm's length was the right one. Sliding into the seat, she locked all the doors before dialing her mother's number.

AT TWO THIRTY IN THE morning, Cash drove his totally hammered friends, Jesse and Boone, through the darkness. He'd known before they left home that he'd be the one making sure they all got safely back to Howelton, so he'd drunk very little at the club.

Boone had turned thirty-three that day and had figured it was a great idea to get roaring drunk. Obviously, Jesse had agreed with him. They'd both given Cash hell all night because he didn't dance and hunt up women the way they did. That just wasn't Cash's style anymore. He'd learned the hard way that party girls didn't make good wives. Misty, his ex, had made him miserable before they divorced. That was a mistake he wouldn't make again.

Cash reached over and shoved Jesse, who was slumped in the passenger seat. His friends frequented The Last Cowboy and should know something about the employees. Especially the pretty ones. "Hey, you know anything about that girl bartending tonight over by the front door? Blond hair and blue eyes?"

Jesse picked his head up and stared blearily at Cash. "Yeah...Dallas. Don't get your hopes up. She don't date guys from the club. Word is she's got a kid. What I hear, she only works weekends." He leaned his head into the side window and closed his eyes.

Cash pursed his lips. What Jesse said made sense. While she waited on customers, Dallas smiled but didn't flirt like a lot of bartenders did.

It had been a long time since a woman had caught his attention. After his divorce, he'd kind of lost interest in dating. He'd tried so hard to make his marriage work, despite the fact that he'd known before their first anniversary that Misty was the wrong woman for him. The things that had first attracted him to her in college had turned into major problems when she became his wife. Accepting full responsibility for his poor choice, he'd done everything in his power to be a good husband. Her long absences from home, however, and, finally, the knowledge that she was sleeping around, had ended their marriage after four long years.

There was something about Dallas, though. It could be her fresh, girl-next-door looks, or her genuine smile, or maybe it was the confidence in the way she moved and talked. Somehow, she was different. He wanted to find out more about her. She didn't date guys from the club? He smiled. He'd see about that.

ETHAN KEYS STRODE TOWARD the break room, eager for his first cup of coffee. His $850 Brunopasso Espresso machine had heaved its last splat of coffee this morning. He frowned. Could he stomach break-room coffee now? Women's voices carried down the hall. One of them sounded like Dallas.

A few steps from the door he overheard her say, "One punch, and he knocked him silly. Then he threw him on the ground. Thank God he was there. I've never been so scared in my life."

Mandy, one of the paralegals, nearly swooned as Ethan walked in.

"A handsome cowboy came to your rescue. Wow! It's like the movies."

What? A cowboy had rescued Dallas? Hold on there. He'd had his eye on Dallas for ages. No way was some cowboy horning in on his turf.

"Hi, ladies. What's up?" He moved over to the coffeepot and sighed sadly as he filled his mug with something very different from what his Brunopasso made him.

Mandy put her arm around Dallas. "The most handsome man in The Last Cowboy Standing rescued this damsel in distress Saturday night." She went on to give him all the details.

Ethan frowned. "Were you hurt? That sounds awful."

Dallas shook her head and rubbed her arm. "Just a few bruises. Thank God Cash was outside getting some fresh air, or I don't know what would have happened."

Though thankful that someone had been there to help Dallas, Ethan didn't care one bit for the excitement in her eyes when she talked about this Cash guy. Working so closely with her for the past three years had given Ethan a proprietary feeling about Dallas. Dammit, he needed to do something about this cowboy business.

If the coffee was as bad as he thought, it would need lots of help to be palatable. He took his time adding cream and sugar to it.

Mandy started back to her desk.

When Dallas followed, he called to her. "Dallas, do you have a second?"

She turned around and smiled. "Sure, but just a sec. I need to get to my desk."

"How about we go out to dinner this week? Maybe make this bad memory go away. Does Wednesday work for you?"

Dallas touched his sleeve. "Oh, thank you for inviting me, Ethan, but Piper was sick all weekend, and she's still on the mend. I need to stay home."

Damn and double damn. He forced an understanding smile and nodded. "Children need their moms when they're not feeling well. Sometime soon, then, okay?" It had been a year since he'd asked her out last. Back then, Dallas had said that at two years old, her daughter was going through a stage where she got upset when her mother left her. So he'd waited all this time to ask her out again. No way would he lose her now to a freaking cowboy.

She nodded. "Sure, Ethan, and thanks again for thinking of me."

He chewed his lip as she walked out the door. With that handsome cowboy on the horizon, he had to step up his game.

He wasn't sure what it was about Dallas that made him so crazy for her. For years he'd watched her at the firm before he'd decided to ask her out. At thirty-five, he knew she was younger—in her mid to late twenties. It had been a long time since he'd dated anyone that young. In fact, in the past few years he'd dated older, wealthy socialites whom he met at the functions he attended through work. Occasionally his mother introduced him to someone in their social set in Dallas as well.

Though he enjoyed their company, Dallas was different—refreshing. She was honest and open. He loved her laugh and that she'd say just about anything. Dallas was beautiful without using a lot of makeup, and he was sure that she was a natural blonde.

She was smart—way too smart to work as an administrative assistant for the rest of her life. One of her team's paralegals had been out on maternity leave recently, and Dallas had shown herself to be so adept at research that her boss, Ethan's business partner, had encouraged her to return to school and become a paralegal herself.

Ethan didn't like her working in that honky-tonk, though. She'd told him that the job funded her school savings, while her work here paid for her living expenses.

As a full partner in the firm, Ethan did very well. He couldn't help but think that if it worked out between them, he could make Dallas's life much easier. She wouldn't have to worry about money, and he would help with her school. He wondered if she ever thought about him in that way. Maybe it was time to drop some hints—make sure she did. After all, he could offer her so much more than any cowboy could.

THE FOLLOWING FRIDAY night, Cash parked in an empty spot near the back of the lot at The Last Cowboy Standing. He let out a loud gust of air. This was a first for him. Two weekends in a row at a honky-tonk? And by himself?

He took the note out of his shirt pocket, reading it for the tenth time. When he'd finished, he sighed. It would have to do. Refolding the paper, he shoved it back in his pocket and opened his door. He couldn't believe the way his heart was pounding. How long had it been since he was nervous about a woman? Ages, that was for sure. He clenched his hands to hold them steady. After the huge mistake he'd made choosing a wife, he had no confidence in his taste in women. *I hope I did a better job this time.* Beeping the locks on his truck, he squared his shoulders and strode toward the entrance.

It was nine o'clock, and the place was just beginning to roll. The band was hammering out the tune of a rowdy North Texas

Red Dirt country song, and dancers were twirling around the floor. Dallas's bar was busy. Standing back, he waited his turn.

As he stepped up to order his beer, Dallas looked at him, eyes wide with surprise. "Cash. You're back."

He smiled. "Yep, I am. How are you?"

"Fine. Um, thanks again about last Saturday night. I really appreciate it."

"You're welcome. Glad I was there to help." He nodded. "Bud Light, please."

When she brought his beer, he handed her a five with his note folded inside it. "Keep the change."

She took the bill and note, a crease between her brows. "Thanks, Cash."

He found a seat not far from the bar, from where he was able to keep an eye on Dallas. Without knowing where she lived or worked, he didn't know what else he could do. The woman was busy as hell in here. Her break was the only time she could talk to him, but he wondered if she called in about her daughter during that time. He didn't want to interfere with that. So the note had been his best idea. It had to work.

THE FIRM EDGES OF THE folded paper poked through Dallas's pocket, reminding her that she couldn't just forget that handsome Cash had come back to the club again tonight. What could he want? The bar had been too busy for her to take the time to read his note. She glanced over at his table. He was still there, watching the dancers out on the floor. Before she could turn away, his gaze swung to her and he grinned. Pressing her lips together, she smiled uneasily, though her heart thudded in response.

A short time later, a pause between customers allowed her to pull the paper out of her pocket and scan it. She felt dizzy as the blood left her face. With trembling fingers, she refolded the note and slipped it back into her pocket. Looking up, and without meaning to, her eyes met Cash's steady gaze. God, he'd watched her read it.

Heat rushed back to her cheeks and she spun around, grabbing a towel and drying the glasses the barback had washed earlier. Cash had asked her out to dinner. The worst thing about it? That flash of joy she'd felt before the stab of fear that had her hands shaking. He was the first man to truly tempt her in the past three years.

Thank God she could practically tend bar with her eyes closed. Her mind flew back to Saturday morning when she'd taken Piper to the grocery store. She'd paused as she'd noticed a man and woman shopping together, each knowing their role, reading the list or taking items from the shelves, and calling the other *honey*. She'd blinked back tears as she passed their cart.

Dallas laid down the towel and opened a bottle of cold water, remembering Tuesday night when, after she'd put Piper to sleep, she'd caught an old rerun of *Pretty Woman*. She'd sobbed out loud at the sappy ending. That night, late as it was, she'd called Sarah, hoping for a clue to her craziness.

Sarah's answer had been as disturbing as Dallas's behavior. She'd said that Dallas should find a man who would give her unconditional love. She'd been scared ever since. Open her heart? Trust a man? Sarah was the crazy one. Yet, a tiny voice inside Dallas had agreed.

While the bar got busy again, Dallas searched her heart for an answer. Letting go of her fear of being hurt didn't feel possible. How did a person just stop being afraid? Start trusting? The only trustworthy man she could think of was her father. He was old-school. Young men didn't seem to have the same capacity. She glanced over at Cash as she handed a woman her beer. Damn. He was looking her way again. Smiling tentatively, she turned to the next person at the bar.

Later, she pulled her phone from her pocket and checked the time. It was getting late, and she was no closer to making a decision than she had been when she'd first read his note.

The pace slowed at around one thirty. She had to decide. Cash didn't dance, and, throughout the evening, he'd bought his beers at the other bar, giving her time to think. She appreciated the consideration, another clue that he was a gentleman.

Admittedly, something had been missing in her life for a while. Much as she hated it, Sarah might have hit it on the head. Maybe that tiny part of her that liked Cash's smile wanted to say yes to the dinner invitation. But, hell, what if this went wrong? Could she handle it? She'd thought the pain from Piper's father's rejection would never go away, and some days it still stabbed at her. She couldn't go through that again.

She looked at Cash's table. He was draining his beer. It was last call, and her time had run out. Ripping a piece of paper from the register, she scribbled quickly as customers headed to the bar.

THE HIGHLINER BAR WAS packed, as per usual, as Dallas arrived during happy hour on Wednesday. She spotted her best friends, Sarah and Kate, sitting, as always, near the middle of the room, where they could keep an eye on everyone coming and going. Dallas sat down and caught the busy waitress's eye, and she swung by the table to take Dallas's drink order.

Kate leaned in. "Sarah and I had time to catch up while we were waiting for you. Tell us what's going on. All of a sudden you're leading an exciting life."

Dallas grinned. "Am not. One rescue from the clutches of death, and you think my life is exciting? Phooey."

The girls rolled their eyes and waited for her to continue.

"Well, Ethan asked me out."

Kate clapped her hands. "Yay! I was hoping he would. He's a wonderful catch for you, Dallas. He moves in all the right circles, makes great money at the firm, and you said he's really nice to you."

"He is. I had to turn him down, though. Piper's little tail was still dragging when he asked."

Kate leaned in and covered Dallas's hand with her own. "Listen, girlfriend, chances like this don't come along every day. Let me remind you how you grew up. No new shoes till your old ones rubbed blisters on your toes. You never had nice clothes like the other kids. Hardly even had enough to eat. Do you want Piper growing up like that? You're putting all your eggs in one basket, counting on finishing your legal degree. Wouldn't it be awesome to just *want* a degree, instead of desperately needing one? Promise me you're going to accept next time he asks."

Dallas swallowed and looked down at her glass of wine, turning it in circles. She still remembered her first day of third grade. One of the bigger boys, who'd always been a bully, had pointed at her old, beat-up tennis shoes with the separated sole. "You wore those things last year, loser. You're poor." Her heart still hurt for the sad little girl she'd been. She couldn't let her daughter go through that. "I know. You're right about never wanting to be poor again. That's why I'm working so hard to get my college fund together. But Ethan really is a sweet guy. Monday he even asked how Piper was feeling."

Sarah held her wine up and they all tapped their glasses. "We're way too serious. I want to hear me some more about that good-looking cowboy."

Dallas smiled and reached into her purse. "You won't believe this, but he came back to the club Friday night. When he paid for his beer, he handed me this note." Unfolding the half-page piece of paper, she held it up.

Sarah gawked at it. "Well go ahead, crazy woman, read it."

Dallas smoothed it a little more, and then read:

Dallas,

I'm here tonight to change your mind. Word is you don't date men you meet at the bar, and I sure don't blame you. Fact is, I wouldn't date girls if I met them there, either.

But I think you and I are exceptions. I was there the night we met for my friend's birthday. I don't normally go to clubs.

I enjoyed meeting you, though I wish it had been under better circumstances.

I'd like to spend a quiet evening together somewhere, get some dinner, and learn more about you. If you're interested, just tell me.

Here's hoping,

Cash

Sarah and Kate both whooshed out, "Wow."

Sarah stared at Dallas and slapped her hand on the table. "Well?"

Dallas fidgeted in her chair. "I didn't know what to do. He seemed so kind, but I never, ever see anyone from the club. You know I don't date, either. But I knew he wouldn't leave until I answered. He came up for his last beer, and I slipped him a note." She took a sip of her wine.

Sarah shook her head, her lips jammed together. "Girl, speak now or I swear—"

Dallas giggled. "I gave him my cell number and thanked him for asking me out."

Sarah threw her arms wide. "Finally, I can't believe it. The girl makes some sense."

"So, when are you having dinner?" Kate asked.

"Tomorrow night, since Piper's feeling okay now. Speaking of my daughter... I gotta scoot. I have so little time with her, what with working and tending bar. Oh, you girls know how I feel guilty, even when I'm in the best of company."

Leaving money for her tab on the table, she kissed each of her friends.

"Get a picture of that cowboy," Sarah called, before Dallas got to the door.

Driving home, she considered Kate's advice. Should she go out with Ethan? It felt weird even considering it. After being a loner for so long, it was hard to imagine that she could be the kind of woman that dressed up and went out on dates.

Yet Ethan had always been sweet to her. And he had a way of making the staff laugh when he dropped by the break room. Though he was hyper-focused with his clients, when he stopped at her desk for a chat, he was easygoing and made Dallas feel like she was the only person in the world. Perhaps if she got through the date with Cash without having a heart attack, she might accept an invitation from Ethan, if he asked again. The strangeness of the situation wasn't lost on her. After swearing off men for years, she'd opened herself to the possibility of dating not one, but two men.

The only thing she hadn't figured out with this whole dating thing was Piper. She had so little time with her daughter. How would she fit dating into her already hectic schedule?

KEEP READING FOR A FREE BOOK OFFER!

GET A FREE BOOK NOW!

At janalynknight.com

ALSO BY JANALYN KNIGHT

Cowboy for a Season
True Blue Texas Cowboy
The Govain Cowboys Series
The Cowboy's Fate
The Cowboy's Choice
The Cowboy's Wish
The Howelton Texas Series
Cowboy Refuge
Cowboy Promise
Cowboy Strong
The Tough Texan Series
Stone One Tough Texan
North Their Tough Texan
Clint Her Tough Texan
The Cowboy SEALs Series
The Cowboy SEAL's Secret Baby
The Cowboy SEAL's Daddy School
The Cowboy SEAL'S Second Chance
The Texas Knights Series
Her Guardian Angel Cowboy
Her Ride or Die Cowboy

DEAR READER

T hank you so much for reading my books. Drop by *jana-lynknight.com*[1] and join my Wranglers Readers Group to be the first to get a look at my newest books and to enter my many giveaways. Or, if you like leaving reviews of the books you read, become a member of my POSSE Review Team at the *Join my POSSE*[2] page on my website and get advance copies of my new books in exchange for leaving honest reviews.

Until next time, may all your dreams be of cowboys!

Janalyn Knight

---

1. *https://janalynknight.com/*

2. *https://janalynknight.com/join-my-posse/*

REVIEW

If you enjoyed Ward's book, please leave a review. Reviews are the life's-blood of an author's living and are very much appreciated!

Please leave your review on Amazon.

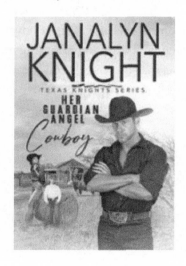

COPYRIGHT

Her Guardian Angel Cowboy, copyright © 2021 by Jana-lyn Knight. This is a work of fiction. Names, places, businesses, characters and incidents are either the product of the author's imagination or are used in a fictitious manner. Any resemblance to actual persons living or dead, actual events or locales is purely coincidental.

About the Author

Nobody knows sexy Texas cowboys like Janalyn. From an early age, she competed in rodeo, later working on a ten-thousand-acre cattle ranch, and these experiences lend an authenticity to her characters and stories. Janalyn is an avid supporter of the Brighter Days Horse Refuge and totally owns the title of wine drinker extraordinaire. When she's not writing spicy cowboy romances, she's living her dream—sharing her twenty-acres of Texas Hill Country with her daughters and their families.

Read more at https://janalynknight.com/.

Made in the USA
Las Vegas, NV
16 March 2022

45774949R00146